CRY
GUILTY

CRY GUILTY

Sara Woods

330 6 7L

ST. MARTIN'S PRESS • NEW YORK

Any work of fiction whose characters were of uniform excellence would rightly be condemned – by that fact if by no other – as being incredibly dull. Therefore no excuse can be considered necessary for the villainy or folly of the people appearing in this book. It seems extremely unlikely that any of them should resemble a real person, alive or dead. Any such resemblance is completely unintentional and without malice.

S.W.

Copyright © 1981 by Sara Woods
For information, write: St. Martin's Press,
175 Fifth Avenue, New York, N.Y. 10010
Manufactured in the United States of America

10 9 8 7 6 5 4 3 2 1
First Edition

Library of Congress Cataloging in Publication Data

Woods, Sara, pseud.
  Cry guilty

  I. Title.
PR6073.063C7 1981   823'.914   80-29319
ISBN 0-312-17802-6

'Now, if you can blush and cry "guilty", cardinal,
You'll show a little honesty.'

King Henry VIII, Act III, Scene ii

PROLOGUE

"I have a client," said Kevin O'Brien, Q.C., and paused there as though the statement were complete in itself. He looked round at his host and hostess, assessing their reaction to the remark. He had more or less invited himself to the Maitlands for a chat after dinner, and the very casualness with which he had done so had been enough to put Antony on his guard. Jenny however, newly returned from their summer vacation and with the unpacking behind her, was as relaxed as a kitten.

"With the Michaelmas term so close upon us," she said, "I should hope you have."

Kevin smiled at the literal way she was treating his remark. He was a thin man, narrow-shouldered, a veteran fighter for lost causes. "I meant one who would be of particular interest to Antony," he told her. "Louise Chorley."

Antony Maitland put down the brandy snifter that he had been cradling between his hands and leaned back in his chair. "Interesting, of course," he said, "but hardly my concern."

"I think it may be," said O'Brien.

"If you're thinking of co-opting me for the defence—"

"Nothing like that."

" — I tell you straight out, I don't think she has one." Maitland was a Queen's Counsel himself, of much the same vintage as O'Brien.

"There's something to be said for the worst of us," said Kevin, and spoke more seriously than was usual with him. "But it sounds as if you were a little more familiar with the matter than the general public are."

"Well, naturally I have a particular interest in it," Antony admitted. "I don't know how you knew that though."

"I didn't. Tell me," O'Brien invited.

"Her husband was about to be arrested for murder when she shot him, and I suppose you might say that was partly

5

my doing," said Maitland reluctantly. "The arrest, I mean, not the shooting."

"And does your knowledge stop there?"

"Well, no. She made a confession, in fact I think she called the police herself."

"And – " prompted O'Brien.

"I had some particulars in confidence of a story she sold to *The Courier*. They can't use it, of course, until after the verdict is in . . . if you're thinking of pleading Not Guilty that is."

"We certainly are."

"I see." His doubtful tone made the words a lie. "Anyway, you don't need to worry, Kevin, the prosecution haven't a hope of getting that admitted in evidence."

"I'm not worried," said Kevin blandly. "I have every intention of introducing it into evidence myself."

Maitland stopped to think that out. Jenny knew as much about the matter as he did, and as it seemed that Kevin O'Brien was also privy to the facts there was nothing to stop him going over them out loud. "The underlying story concerned a ring of art thieves, into which her husband had been co-opted. She said the man on top, the instigator of the whole thing, whatever you like to call him, had been her lover for years. She was afraid her husband would talk, would give this man away, and that's why she shot him." He paused and looked at the visitor doubtfully. "Do you really think that that would make either judge or jury more sympathetic towards Mrs Chorley?" he asked.

"Not the way you tell it. Our story will be that she's as mad as a hatter, and that the whole story is a pure invention on her part. Not Guilty, by reason of insanity."

"Yes," said Maitland slowly, "I can see that's the only line you can take."

"It would have occurred to you too if you'd been lumbered with her as a client," said Kevin kindly. "And in case it worries you, Jenny, her story just isn't believable as she tells it, and she's never shown the slightest trace of sanity during our interviews. Not that she's raving, of course. But that wasn't what I wanted to talk to Antony about."

6

"You're not wanting my evidence?" said Antony, alarmed.

"Nothing like that. There seems no reason why either prosecution or defence should want to go into David Chorley's crimes at all, except for a bare statement from the police that an arrest was imminent. It was hearing about that that snapped my client's rather tenuous hold on reality," said O'Brien, so solemnly that Maitland knew at once it was his brief speaking.

"Thank goodness for that anyway. Nobody knew of my connection with the Selden case, and I'd rather keep it that way."

"If you're talking about that affair where a medium was charged with fraud—"

"And had a whacking great sum claimed against her in damages because a woman named Emily Walpole had committed suicide, supposedly because of something she'd been told at a seance," said Antony. "And then it turned out that Mrs Walpole had been murdered after all."

"Yes, but that was Sir Nicholas's case," O'Brien objected.

"I had a hand in it too."

"I might have known." O'Brien sounded more resigned than anything else. "Anyway, this is nothing to do with the Selden case either. I hear through the grapevine," said Kevin, "that you have a client too."

"Like you, I suppose, several. But you're referring to one in particular, aren't you? Which is it?"

"A lad called Alan Kirby." He saw Maitland's puzzled look, and added a little impatiently, "Haven't you even been into chambers since you came back from the vacation?"

"Yes, of course I have. I was anxious to see what horrors Mallory had accepted on my behalf while we were away. But Alan Kirby . . . that wasn't anything very important, as far as I remember. A charge of receiving stolen goods."

"Have you seen your client?"

"No, just the brief from Geoffrey Horton. The police obviously didn't think they could make a charge of theft stick."

7

"Well," said O'Brien, speaking patiently as though to a child, "what stolen goods is he accused of receiving?"

"A painting, I think, stolen from the Sefton Gallery. I haven't been into the matter thoroughly yet, it's a fair way down the list as far as I can make out. And Kirby's out on bail, Geoffrey arranged that."

"You're not using your head, Antony." Maitland had got up restlessly while they were speaking, and was now standing with his back to the grate where the fire was laid but not lighted. Like O'Brien, he was a tall man, dark, with a thin, intelligent face, and a humorous look that was generally very marked, but which he found it politic to suppress on official occasions. "An art theft," said O'Brien impressively. "Since you know so much about what happened last March, haven't you connected the two things in your own mind?"

"You just said—"

"Forget the Seldens and the Walpoles and the whole lot of them except the Chorleys. And accept the fact that there's a gang operating who specialise in art thefts."

"Are you trying to tell me that Kirby might be the missing lover? I must point out he's only in his middle twenties, and an historian, I believe, not an art expert," said Maitland, whose cursory reading of his brief had obviously made more of an impression on him than he had been willing to admit.

"I'm trying to tell you the exact opposite. He may be completely innocent. What else do you know about him?"

"He's of good character, as they say, never been in trouble of any sort. No, really, Kevin, I haven't had time to take it all in yet. And if you think I'm taking the matter lightly," he added a little stiffly, "I'm quite aware of what a conviction could mean for him, if he is in fact innocent."

"I never thought otherwise," said Kevin soothingly.

"Well, what makes you think he's innocent?" Antony demanded.

"Something Louise Chorley said."

"As you practically invited yourself here this evening,"

8

said Maitland disagreeably, "I suppose you're going to tell me what that was."

"Certainly I am. She'd heard about the charge, and she said it was all nonsense, Alan would never do a thing like that. It was one of the few lucid things, may I tell you, that she said during the whole time I was with her. But considering the claim she made I thought she might be in a position to know, so I made a few enquiries."

"And what did these enquiries of yours elicit?"

"Alan Kirby has an uncle, Daniel of the same name, who is said to have the best private collection of art in Britain, if you exclude the Royal collection."

"Is he on good terms with his nephew?" Maitland's tone was sharper now.

"Yes, I think so."

"You're implying that Daniel Kirby might be Mrs Chorley's lover. Wouldn't that make it more rather than less likely that his nephew might be one of his agents?"

"I can only tell you what she said, and a very distinct impression I got that, at that moment, she was telling me the truth as she saw it. She clammed up then, wouldn't say another word. But I thought you ought to know."

"The woman is your client, O'Brien."

"The trouble with you, Maitland," said Kevin, becoming formal in his turn, "is that you're too damned ethical."

"That may be so, though I don't think everyone I know would agree with you. But you're telling me you believe her story – the story she sold for hard cash to *The Courier* – and not all this business about her being Not Guilty by reason of insanity?"

"I happen to believe in your discretion, Antony." O'Brien looked at Jenny and his expression softened. "There are people I'd defend for nothing," he said, "but Louise Chorley isn't one of them." Antony had the thought that perhaps in the whole world Jenny was the only person whose opinion the other man valued sufficiently to have made that explanation. "All the same," Kevin went on, "I shall follow my instructions from Bellerby. They are as I've explained them to you, and that's that." (Mr Bellerby was a solicitor, well known to Maitland, whose advocacy of a

9

policy of kindness towards clients was renowned among his brethren in the senior branch of the profession, and often very annoying to them.)

"But if you're right...if Louise Chorley was indeed telling you the truth, how did this ruddy great painting get into Alan Kirby's possession?"

"That's up to you. Someone might have asked him to store it for them, for instance," said Kevin vaguely.

"If that was so, I think Geoffrey Horton would have heard of it."

"Unless there's some family loyalty involved," O'Brien pointed out. "It's up to you what you do about this, Antony," he went on; though he knew well enough, Jenny reflected a little ruefully, what the outcome would be. "But if I were you I'd have at least one interview with him before you get into court."

"I intend to," said Antony, and shivered suddenly. "Goose walking over my grave," he apologised, looking at his wife. "All the same, Jenny love, don't you think it would be a good idea to put a match to the fire?"

"If you like." Jenny hadn't changed her position, and she sounded calm enough, but he was aware all at once of a little strain behind the words. It was only later, when the fire was blazing merrily, a second helping of the cognac usually reserved for Sir Nicholas's use had been consumed, and O'Brien had left them, that she spoke her mind. "I know you said nobody knew of your connection with the Selden case, Antony, but don't you think Louise Chorley would have told her lover about the questions you were asking?"

"Kevin says he doesn't exist," said Antony, as lightly as he could.

"Yes, but he doesn't believe it, and I don't think you do either. If he, whoever he is—and it's quite possible he's this Daniel Kirby that Kevin was talking about—knows you're taking even more interest in his affairs, don't you think he might resent it?"

Antony, back in his favourite place on the hearth-rug, looked down at her with affection. Jenny had gravitated to one corner of the sofa when the room was first furnished, and a vainer person might have been suspected of having

10

chosen deliberately to sit where the lamplight fell on her brown curls, gilding them in a most becoming way. But nobody who knew Jenny could have entertained that thought for an instant; she was as completely unself-conscious as it is possible for a member of the human race to be. "I only said I'd talk to my client," Antony pointed out gently.

"Yes, but... I don't think Uncle Nick would like it," said Jenny, playing her trump card. Sir Nicholas Harding was Antony's uncle, the head of the chambers to which he belonged in the Inner Temple, and the owner of the house in Kempenfeldt Square in which Antony and Jenny occupied the two top floors as a far-from-self-contained flat. It was not much more than a year since Sir Nicholas had married, after a lifetime of bachelorhood, Miss Vera Langhorne, barrister-at-law. Antony, who was inclined – or so most of his friends would have told you – to see difficulties where none existed, had felt that might be the time for the parting of the ways. Fortunately for everyone's peace of mind circumstances had convinced him otherwise before he did anything irrevocable; except when Sir Nicholas – not the most even-tempered of men – was in one of his moods, the household had always been a happy one, and Vera's arrival had made it no less so. In fact, Jenny would have told you that the new Lady Harding had an influence over her husband's small staff that nobody else had ever attempted to exercise before, and that things were much more comfortable in consequence...

"Uncle Nick would approve of my carrying out my professional duties as well as I can," said Antony firmly.

"Even if they lead to trouble?" asked Jenny.

"You know," said Antony, after a moment's thought, "if you put it to him squarely, I think even then. Of course, he'd carry on something frightful, but we're used to that, aren't we?" He turned away from her and regarded the fire for a moment, almost as though he were reading a message there. "I really don't think you need worry, love," he said then. "This idea of Kevin's, it's all a nonsense. Anyway, there's no reason why Uncle Nick should ever hear a word about it."

"Uncle Nick hears everything," said Jenny flatly.

11

He turned to look at her then. "Yes, I know he does. His friend, Bruce Halloran, has the best intelligence service in the profession. But that doesn't matter, after all. What does matter, Jenny, is that you're worrying, and that worries me. But I don't think there's the slightest need."

"Perhaps not," agreed Jenny docilely. She didn't mention the subject again that night, but her husband was under no illusions that it had been altogether banished from her mind.

PART I

MICHAELMAS TERM, 1972

Friday, 29th September

Geoffrey Horton was inclined to be fretful when Maitland asked for an interview with his client, Alan Kirby. "If you'd only read your brief," he protested.

"I have," Antony told him, and for once in his life this was true.

"I know you've a weakness for hearing things at first hand," Geoffrey went on, ignoring the comment, "but in this case it can't do any good. The whole defence doesn't amount to a row of beans."

"You mean we're guilty?"

"Those are not my instructions," said Horton precisely. "However, what I mean is there isn't a thing we can say for him in court. If they were trying to prove theft that would have been a different matter, something we could get our teeth into, but receiving stolen goods... the picture was there in his room, it was certainly stolen, and what can we do in the face of that?"

"I'd still like to see him," said Antony stubbornly.

"Oh, very well! I'll do what I can," said Geoffrey, still in a grumbling tone. But Maitland wasn't surprised when his friend telephoned later in the day, to say that a meeting had been fixed up for the following morning.

Maitland's room in chambers was long and narrow and inclined to be shadowy even on the most sunny day. When he had first taken it over Jenny had offered to come in and paint the walls a more cheerful colour, and perhaps complement them with some new curtains, but this Sir Nicholas had strictly vetoed. Even Antony would have been the first to admit that there were occasions when it was a good thing that there was nothing in his surroundings to distract his mind, it was hard enough in any case to concentrate. That Friday morning when Willett, who was by now second in seniority to old Mr Mallory himself, showed the two visitors into the room, Antony was wishing with all his heart that he'd never allowed Kevin O'Brien to talk him into this lunacy. He could see no good

15

likely to come of it, and the uneasiness which his talk with Kevin had engendered had long since worn off.

Geoffrey Horton had red hair, darkened over the years by the application of oil in a vain attempt to stop it from waving. His disposition was normally cheerful, but professionally he was a stickler for the conventions, and it cannot be denied that Maitland's unorthodox ways had at times been a trial to him, though perhaps it would be an exaggeration to say that it had strained their friendship, which was of long standing. On this particular morning his manner was perhaps a little over-hearty; he was far too old a hand to be shocked by anything his client might or might not have done, but he could see nothing that could be accomplished for him, and didn't want to raise his hopes unduly as he feared this conference might.

While the introductions were being made, Antony was taking stock of the man about whose chances of acquittal his instructing solicitor was so pessimistic. Alan Kirby, he had already informed himself, was twenty-five years of age, a man of medium height with brown hair, brown eyes, and a healthy tan. On top of this he was wearing a brown suit, and had chosen a tie in which autumn colours predominated. Altogether a little too neat, a little too well turned out, and Antony wondered whether this was natural, or whether it had been done to impress his counsel.

The chairs provided for visitors were nothing to write home about. Geoffrey moved his a little nearer the window, as though dissociating himself from the whole affair, but as this left the client with the one nearer the desk, where the light of the lamp fell directly on his face, Maitland had no fault to find. In fact he was perfectly well aware that Geoffrey had arranged things that way. "I'm sorry to put you to the trouble of coming here, Mr Kirby," he said, when they had all seated themselves, "but when Mr Horton and I discussed the matter we came to the conclusion that it would be as well for me to see you."

"I don't know much about the way these things are handled," said Kirby. "Nothing like this has ever happened to me before, you see." He had a pleasant manner, and if

16

he was trying rather too hard to make a good impression that was hardly to be wondered at.

"In a case like this, where matters seem fairly straight-forward – " said Antony vaguely, and did not attempt to finish the sentence. Then he smiled. "But Mr Horton will tell you I'm a great trial to him, I have a weakness for hearing things for myself."

"But that's just it." Alan Kirby's tone was more eager now, he seemed to be forgetting his self-consciousness. "It isn't straightforward at all! I mean, I haven't the faintest idea how the thing got into my room."

"We'll come to that in a moment. First I want you to tell me something about yourself."

"There's nothing very interesting about me," Kirby warned him. "I'm not of a very practical turn of mind, so I read history at University. I'd like to write myself, but that takes time for the necessary research, and meanwhile there's the little matter of keeping the wolf from the door. So I work for the Holiday Press, one of their editors."

"Holiday Press?" said Antony, with an enquiring look at Horton. He could almost see the words, It's all in the brief, hovering on the solicitor's tongue. "They aren't general publishers," said Geoffrey. "In fact, I connect them with greeting cards mostly."

"You wouldn't write the verses for those?" said Antony, and was relieved when Kirby returned his smile, which had been quite involuntary, without taking offence.

"No, I'm afraid I couldn't aspire to that. Mr Horton's forgotten one or two matters: they do cookbooks too, and books about gardening, and matters of local historical interest. That's where I come in. I don't mean local in the sense of just concerning London of course; any district will do, and that's where my articles will be mainly advertised and sold."

"That's very interesting," said Antony seriously. Kirby gave him a quick, rather suspicious look, before he realised that his counsel meant exactly what he said.

"It may seem so to an outsider," said Alan, "but I assure you that, as a day-to-day job, I can think of things I'd rather be doing."

17

"Yes, I've no doubt about that. Your family now, what about them?"

"My parents died years ago, some bug they picked up abroad. I was brought up by my uncle. He and his wife are the only relations I have, except for a cousin of Aunt Hilda's. That would make her a connection by marriage, I expect."

"I have an uncle myself," said Antony, hoping to encourage him to further confidences. "And though there are occasions when I consider him a mixed blessing, on the whole I must say I approve of him."

"I've heard of Sir Nicholas Harding," said Alan, and grinned in his turn. "I'm fond of my uncle and aunt, of course, they've been endlessly good to me, but I think on the whole it's Aunt Hilda I'm closer to. She has a motherly nature, and no children of her own."

"This must all seem very trivial to you, Mr Kirby, but I should like to know what your uncle does for a living, for instance."

"Oh, he's retired. Not that he need have done, I mean he's nowhere near the age that most men work to, but Grandfather left him well placed financially, so there was no need for him to go on."

"Your own father didn't benefit from your grandfather's will?"

"No, it was rather strangely worded, left everything to the surviving brother. Aunt Hilda always says Grandfather meant to change it after my father died, I don't know whether that was true or not. Anyway I haven't a penny, except what I earn."

"Have you ever resented that fact?"

"No, I don't think I have."

"Then you're something of a paragon, aren't you? It seems a very inequitable arrangement to me."

Kirby's whole attention was riveted on his counsel, otherwise he would have seen the quick, enquiring look that Horton threw in Maitland's direction. "If I had money," said Alan steadily, "I'd be doing what I want instead of a hack job, and probably enjoying life more. But it hasn't happened that way, and I've plenty of cause to be grateful to Uncle Dan."

18

"A most damnable emotion," said Maitland, more sympathetically. "Was it from him you learned your love of art?"

"I'd every opportunity of doing so." Alan didn't seem to find the question odd. "Unfortunately the whole subject is a closed book to me, Aunt Hilda and I are a pair really in that respect, a great disappointment to Uncle Dan."

"I see. I hope when we get into court, Mr Kirby, you can convey your lack of resentment to the jury as well as you've done to me." Geoffrey Horton had a puzzled look, but Alan Kirby relaxed visibly at his tone. "Do you still live with Mr and Mrs Kirby?"

"Not since I came down. And, of course, when I was up at Oxford I was only home during the vacations. I think Aunt Hilda was a little hurt when I left, but I really felt it was the best thing to do."

"Your uncle didn't share her emotion then?"

"I don't think he cared either way."

"Where do you live now?"

"In digs. An enormous house in Earls Court run by a Mrs Campbell. She gives us breakfast, and dinner if we want it, and the rooms aren't really too bad."

"Whereabouts is your room?"

"On the first floor at the front. It has the advantage of being near the bathroom. It's furnished as a bed-sitter, really quite comfortable," he repeated, as though he didn't want them to be in any doubt about that.

"Then I think we've reached the point when I must ask you to tell me exactly what happened when the painting was found in your room. You must realise that one of the things we must explain to the jury is how it came about that you didn't notice it, if you were not in fact responsible for its being there."

"I wasn't, I told Mr Horton that."

"Then try your explanation on me," Maitland suggested.

"It wasn't a framed painting, you know. Rather a large canvas, but rolled up and pushed to the back of my wardrobe at the bottom. It's one of those enormous ones, the wardrobe, I mean, and I shovel all sorts of things in

19

there out of sight. It was really no wonder I didn't notice that anything had been added to the muddle."

"Tell me what happened," Antony repeated.

"Two plain-clothes men came round one evening. Do you want dates?"

"They're not important at the moment." He paused to smile at Geoffrey. "Besides, Mr Horton has already provided me with them."

"Well, I was quite astonished of course. Mrs Campbell called me down to the hall to speak to them, and though she went back to her own room I'm quite sure she didn't shut the door. They told me they were acting on information received, but when I asked them they wouldn't tell me any more than that. And they hadn't got a warrant, but they said it would save a lot of trouble all round if I'd give them permission to take a look at my room. And, like a fool, I consented."

"It was reasonable enough from their point of view. They couldn't have got a warrant in any case without some more substantial evidence. If they'd been offered any Mr Horton would have heard about that after you were arrested, but apparently all they had was an anonymous phone call. And as you were so compliant, of course it saved them a lot of bother."

"I had no reason not to be, I do assure you of that. All the same I can see," he added, "that if I'd been guilty I'd have done just the same thing. Otherwise they'd have been bound to be suspicious."

"I was just thinking the same thing myself," said Maitland cordially. "Whatever you did, the prosecution could make it sound suspicious, so the only thing to do would have been to brazen it out. So they went upstairs, and you went with them I suppose, and they searched your room, and finally they came to the wardrobe."

"As a matter of fact that was the first place they looked. They were perfectly polite about it, you know. And when they pulled out this great long thing – it looked like a tube of some sort – I couldn't believe my eyes. I knew I'd never put anything like that in there."

"What happened then?"

"They unrolled it and showed it to me. Did I recognise

20

it? Of course, I had to say I didn't. The only paintings I know anything about are portraits, historical likenesses, and that's not for the artistic value but for the interest of seeing what the people I read about looked like."

"As a matter of interest, what was the subject of this painting?"

"I don't remember very well. Three nude women, with a lot too much flesh. One was dipping her toe into a pond, and looked exactly as though she was finding the water too cold. I didn't see anything in it, but Uncle Dan said – "

"We're getting ahead of our story. What happened next?"

"They took it away with them. And then they came back to say it had been identified by the owner of the Sefton Gallery as a Rubens that had been stolen from him three months before."

"And so you were arrested?"

"Yes, I was. I didn't know any solicitors, it was Aunt Hilda who suggested Mr Horton to me." He turned a little to look at Geoffrey. "She seemed to have heard of you," he added.

"I'm grateful for her recommendation," said Geoffrey formally. "How did your uncle and aunt take all this, Mr Kirby?"

"I'm thankful to say they don't think I've done anything wrong. Aunt Hilda wouldn't anyway, and Uncle Dan just says I'd never have had the good taste to select a painting like that." For the first time he looked almost amused. "He's not too wrong at that. It's the last thing I'd want to live with."

"My impression is," said Geoffrey, turning to Maitland, "that the police think Mr Kirby committed the theft as well, only they haven't a shred of proof so they haven't accused him of that."

"I suppose, from their point of view, that's reasonable. And this brings us to the difficult part, Mr Kirby. If you didn't steal the painting, or receive it illegally, how did it get into your wardrobe?"

"There's only one answer to that: I haven't the faintest idea."

"You didn't put it there yourself, to store it for a friend

21

perhaps, who gave you a specious account of why he couldn't keep it for himself at the moment?"

"Nothing like that. I'm not quite sure . . . Mr Maitland, are you suggesting I should say something like that in court?"

"Not unless it's true. You'll be under oath, remember. But if that isn't what happened we're left with the uncomfortable fact that somebody deliberately framed you. Do you know of anybody who has a grudge against you?"

"Nobody at all."

"Or who could have any other reason for wanting to put the painting in that particular place?"

"I tell you . . . .no!"

"A matter of expediency then," said Maitland thoughtfully. "Though that doesn't seem altogether likely, in view of the fact that somebody apparently informed the police that it was there. Have you any idea why that was done, Geoffrey?"

"Not the least idea in the world."

"Well then! That's one point to work on, motive. The other is even more obvious . . . opportunity."

"I suppose you mean, who could have put it there? The door of the house is open from about eight o'clock in the morning until Mrs Campbell retires to watch television after dinner."

"You're telling me *anybody* could have got in?"

"Wait a bit," said Geoffrey. "Mr Kirby was mentioned by name in the telephone call, that means the painting could only have been planted by someone who knew where his room was."

"In any case it would have been difficult," said Alan hesitantly. "Mrs Campbell suffers from arthritis, and hardly ever leaves the house. She has a girl to help her, a niece I believe, who does all the shopping. And she likes to know what's going on – I'm back with Mrs Campbell now – so she's very much inclined to pop out into the hall when she hears the front door. Of course it'd be possible to hit upon a moment when she wasn't within ear-shot, but anybody who'd ever visited me would most likely have encountered her."

22

"Yes, and one would feel a little self-conscious wandering in with a great roll of canvas under one's arm," Maitland agreed. "And before we go any further with this, I'm forgetting one point. The painting was stolen three months before it was found in your quarters; could it have been there all the time?"

"No, not possibly. I've thought about this a lot, of course. I was looking for a book I had about old inns in Sussex; someone else had written on the same subject, and submitted it to Holiday Press, so I thought it would be useful to see what had been done already, whether they covered the same ground. I can't remember the exact date, but I must have been ferreting about in the bottom of the wardrobe not more than a week before the police came. I couldn't have helped but see the canvas if it had been there."

"We'd better get down to dates then."

It was Geoffrey Horton who answered. "Apparently the phone call was made on the morning of the fifth of September. That was a Tuesday, if it's relevant at all. I think – and this is guesswork, Antony – that they took it more seriously because Mr Daniel Kirby is such a very famous collector."

"And, of course, because of the rash of art thefts they've been investigating lately."

"Yes, that's true. Anyway they went round to see our client that very evening."

"Thank you, that's very helpful, even if we are both guessing. Then you were looking for this book during the last week in August, were you, Mr Kirby?"

"I can't remember the exact date, but it certainly was during that week."

"At the beginning of the week perhaps?"

"No, I remember now, it was on the Friday, because I found the book and it was more interesting than I expected and I read it in bed until rather late that night. I remember thinking it didn't matter, because of the next day being Saturday."

Geoffrey produced a pocket diary and handed it silently to Maitland. "I make that the first of September then," he said.

"Do you think that would be right?"

"Yes, I'm sure of it now," said Alan positively.

"Were you at home that weekend?"

"I'd have to think about that. In the sense that I slept there, yes, certainly. But it isn't the kind of place . . . well there's not much inducement to stay in, especially if it happened to be fine weather. If I stayed in it would be because . . . wait a bit now! That Saturday was the morning Ray called me, in fact the telephone woke me up."

"You're going to have to explain Ray."

"Raymond Shields, my employer. He owns Holiday Press."

"And this telephone call you had from him helps you to remember—?"

"Yes, it sets the scene for me. He isn't a man to take much account of weekends, and he was anxious about the manuscript I mentioned to you, and wanted to know whether I advised going ahead with it. Normally I could have given him a straight yes or no, and the book I already had on the same subject should have clinched matters. But there were a few new points, it was very interestingly presented. We talked about that for a bit, and finally he decided to come round and see me."

"So you stayed in at least until he came?"

"I told you I was getting the picture more clearly now. He came about eleven o'clock." He paused again, and again there was a look of amusement. "But not, I assure you, with the ruddy great canvas the police found under his arm."

"No, that would be too much to expect. Had he visited you at home before?"

"No, that was the first time."

"Were you at all surprised at his decision to come?"

"Not a bit, Ray's an impulsive person, something occurs to him and he does it, that's all."

"So at least this visit told him exactly where your room was situated."

"Yes, it did, but it's ridiculous to think—"

"I'm not thinking anything at this stage," said Maitland flatly. "I'm looking for information, that's all."

24

"As long as you understand – " Again he left the sentence uncompleted.

"I understand that you're pleading Not Guilty. That being so you must allow me to...explore avenues, shall we say?" At that moment Maitland's humorous look was very apparent, and his client responded for the first time with open amusement.

"Then if I tell you Aunt Hilda came to tea that afternoon you won't jump to the conclusion that she planted the canvas on me," he said. "I told you it was all becoming clear to me, and there's another thing. Mrs Campbell was away that weekend."

"So what you told me about her watchfulness wouldn't apply?"

"No, it wouldn't. Nancy was there, of course, she might have seen something. But why I remember so clearly is that I made a joke to Bernard that it was a pity that it was Aunt Hilda and not some bright young thing I was entertaining. Mrs Campbell is very strict about that kind of thing, you see. And if that's your next question, Aunt Hilda has been there several times before, and even Uncle Dan had come with her occasionally."

"Does your new-found memory extend to the rest of the day?"

"Yes, I went out to dinner with Bernard and Jackie in the evening. They both live at Mrs Campbell's too, and we've become friends."

"Have you got their full names, Geoffrey?"

"No, it didn't seem material."

"I'd like to have them, all the same." He looked enquiringly at Alan Kirby.

"Jacqueline Gardiner and Bernard Ramsey," said Alan promptly.

"How many people are there at Mrs Campbell's altogether?"

"Besides the three of us, only Mr Brewster on the ground floor. One of the rooms down there, as I told you, is the dining-room; he has the other; and Mrs Campbell and the girl use the kitchen as their sitting-room, as well as for its normal purpose."

"And upstairs?"

"I have one room on the first floor, and Jackie and Bernard have the others. Jackie's is at the back, and much smaller. Mrs Campbell has the whole of the top floor."

"What can you tell me about Mr Brewster?"

"He's about a hundred and ten, and goes out even less than Mrs Campbell does."

"Do you know him at all? Have you done anything to offend him, for instance?"

"We see each other at meals sometimes, I'm sure he couldn't have anything against me. In any case, as I told you, he's practically moribund."

"Any occupation?"

"He must have had one, I suppose, but he's retired by now."

"And the other two lodgers are friends of yours?"

"Very good friends." He sounded a little affronted, and again Antony smiled at him.

"You mustn't mind my questions," he said. "I have to find out, you see, who could have known which room you occupy."

"Well, everybody in the house did, of course."

Maitland fumbled in his pocket until he found a rather tattered envelope, on which he proceeded to make some illegible-looking notes. "And Mr Shields knew, and your aunt and uncle," he said. "Do you do much entertaining?"

"None at all, except for Aunt Hilda occasionally. Most of the people I'd have wanted to invite would have been on Mrs Campbell's forbidden list, so it was much easier to meet outside."

"Then the people you've mentioned are the only ones who know exactly which room you occupy?"

"Yes, I think . . . no, I'm forgetting Ernest Connolly."

"Who is he?"

"One of the editors on *The Courier*. I was writing a series for them in my spare time, in fact I still am, about historic London. Before I started he came round to discuss it. But that was weeks ago."

"I can tell from your tone what you think of my questions," Maitland told him. "What do *you* think happened, Mr Kirby? Assuming your own innocence, as we seem to be doing for the purposes of this discussion."

"I suppose the answer to that is, I don't know, it's a complete mystery to me."

"But you must have thought about it," Maitland insisted.

"Of course I have. I've thought of very little else, and not got anywhere at all. None of the people I've mentioned would have done such a thing, where would they have got the canvas from in any case?"

"The Rubens painting, as I'm sure you'll hear it referred to more often in court, was stolen," Antony pointed out.

"Well, that's just as ridiculous. In any case, even if one of them went mad and did such a thing, why should they plant it on me?"

"That's the greatest puzzle of all." Maitland turned to look at his instructing solicitor, and caught a momentary look of alarm. "So we're left with this position, Mr Kirby: if we assume that the same person planted the canvas and made the telephone call to the police – and it's difficult to see how anyone else would have had the necessary knowledge – we're left with a limited number of people who knew exactly which room you occupy. The painting wasn't in your wardrobe on Friday evening the first of September, and you yourself were at home until after tea on the Saturday. Am I right about that?"

"Yes, quite right."

"But at any time after that, until the visit of the police on the evening of the fifth, you were at home very little?"

"I was in and out all day on the Sunday."

"But Mrs Campbell wasn't there at the weekend to act as watchdog. I've no alternative but to act on the facts as I know them, but I must ask you to think very carefully whether anybody else might have known exactly where you live, or whether someone you haven't thought of so far might have a grudge against you and therefore have made it his business to find out."

"What are you going to do?" Alan Kirby sounded definitely uneasy, and Geoffrey allowed himself a private smile in sympathy.

27

"Ask questions," said Maitland laconically. "Make a nuisance of myself to all your friends and relations. But I haven't finished with you yet, Mr Kirby."

"What else can you possibly want to know?"

"A very simple question really. Do you know Louise Chorley?"

For a moment Alan Kirby just stared at him open-mouthed. "What on earth can that have to do with all this?" he asked.

"Perhaps nothing. Perhaps everything," said Maitland enigmatically. Geoffrey was staring at him too. "All the same, I should like an answer to my question."

"Well, of course I know her. For one thing, she was a good friend of Aunt Hilda's. Of Uncle Dan's too, of course, but she had more in common with my aunt. You can imagine the kind of stir it caused when she was arrested for shooting her husband."

"Did you know him too?" Anthony's tone was casual.

"Yes, in the way one does know people of another generation."

"You said 'for one thing', as if there was some other reason you should have known her."

"Well, of course, Holiday Press published her poems. I don't mean I had anything to do with them," he added hastily, "but I did see her around the office a few times."

"I remember now, I was told she wrote optimistic little verses for the newspapers. You're not telling me she did those things on the greeting cards too?"

"No, nothing like that. Though I don't see much difference myself. Ray used to make collections of her poems and put them out in time for Christmas. I think people used them instead of cards sometimes, though it was rather an expensive way of sending good wishes."

" *The Courier* wouldn't have been one of the newspapers she wrote for, would it?"

"Yes, as a matter of fact it was. They'd shove one of the poems in when they had a space to fill, I remember Mr Connolly complaining about it. Apparently his wife was one of Mrs Chorley's sincerest admirers."

"I must have seen them then, and some sense of self-preservation prevented me reading them." Maitland made one last note and came to his feet. "I think I needn't trouble you any further, Mr Kirby," he said formally. "But if you could wait a few minutes, Geoffrey, I'd like a word with you."

He had pressed the bell on his desk, and almost before he finished speaking the door opened and Willett appeared. He was the one of the clerks who identified himself most closely with Maitland's affairs, which Antony sometimes felt was a good thing, considering that old Mr Mallory had never become completely reconciled to his ways. "Will you show Mr Kirby out, Willett?" he asked now. And thanked his client again for his co-operation before Alan left, still looking rather stunned.

It was obvious that Geoffrey Horton had difficulty in containing himself until the door was safely shut. "What the hell do you mean by bringing Louise Chorley's name into this?" he demanded.

Antony sat down again in a leisurely way, which, though he didn't realise it, was an echo of his uncle's manner. "You may as well stay and we'll go to lunch together," he said, ignoring the question. "If you've no other engagement, that is."

"Nothing else, but that doesn't answer my question," said Geoffrey, annoyed.

"I'd better explain."

"Yes, I think that would be best." Horton's tone was a little grim.

"Louise Chorley doesn't think Alan Kirby is guilty," said Antony, and proceeded to recount the relevant part of his talk with O'Brien, though omitting all reference to Kevin's plan of campaign for the defence of his client. "So I thought it might be as well to see him," he concluded.

"A slim enough reason, if you ask me." Geoffrey was not yet placated. "And half way through you suddenly decided he was innocent, and I can't see the reason for that either."

"Now how on earth did you know that? Not that you're altogether right; it did occur to me, but I wouldn't say I was completely free from doubts."

"I could tell from your manner," said Geoffrey. "I've never yet known you get rough with a client unless you're

29

inclined to believe his story. But I still say it's ridiculous, Antony. The whole thing *could* have been a plant, but why should anybody want to get Kirby into trouble?"

"Why, indeed?"

"The painting's valuable – if you care to look through the papers I sent you you'll see exactly how valuable – so that makes it even more unlikely."

"I'll admit that the point you make is the most interesting one of all, and also the one that is likely to give us the most trouble in court. I shall have to see the people in the boarding-house, of course," said Antony meditatively, "but did you notice that, of the other people who knew where our client's room is situated, every one of them has some connection with Mrs Chorley?"

"What difference does that make?"

"That's something that isn't yet public knowledge, but I think perhaps I can tell you in confidence, particularly as Kevin O'Brien is quite prepared for it to be admitted into evidence when the trial comes on. She sold her story to *The Courier,* and the most interesting point of all is the reason she gave for shooting her husband."

"What was that, for heaven's sake?" Geoffrey still sounded grumpy.

"You heard all about the ring of art thieves when we were acting for Mrs Selden," said Antony. "Mrs Chorley says the – the organiser, if I can put it that way, had been her lover for years. She was afraid David Chorley might talk out of turn if he were arrested, and did what she did to protect the other man."

"That's fantastic!"

"Interesting, certainly."

"I suppose you're going to tell me next that one of these men who have been mentioned this morning was the lover concerned," said Geoffrey. "It's the wildest of guesses, but if you happen to be right I think it would be damn foolish to get mixed up in the matter at all."

"You're getting ahead of me, Geoffrey. I've no opinion at all in the matter yet." He glanced again at his envelope, and stuffed it back into his pocket. "I don't know anything about Shields or Connolly at the moment, but don't you think Daniel Kirby would be a good candidate for the post

30

we're talking about?" he said, apparently not realising he was giving the lie to his previous statement. "I've been told he has one of the best private collections of art in the country."

"I can see it's quite hopeless arguing with you," said Geoffrey. "There's an organiser of all these thefts, you say, and people working for him."

"If you remember, that's what Detective Chief Inspector Sykes told me."

"Then the most likely thing is that Alan Kirby is one of his minions. Though I admit," he added, after a moment's thought, "there's a difference in the method that was used."

"How do you mean?"

"David Chorley took the whole thing, frame and all. The Rubens had been slit neatly from its frame and removed that way."

"I expect that was the only way of dealing with it, short of hiring a removal van and crew. Anyway, Geoffrey, as you say, the real puzzle is why Alan Kirby should have been selected as a scapegoat, and who hated him enough to sacrifice a valuable picture in the cause?"

"You really do think he's innocent then?"

"I said I still had a lingering doubt, but I do feel there's a case for investigation. And how many times have I said that to you, Geoffrey, since we first met?"

"Dozens I should think, and you haven't always been right," Horton reminded him. "But in this case I can see one big difficulty. It's all very well for us to talk to the people who live in Kirby's lodging-house, they might conceivably know something that would help him. But what are we going to say to these other people, whom I suppose are the ones you really want to see?"

Antony grinned at him. "We?" he said.

"My company would give some semblance of propriety at least to your actions," said Horton stiffly.

"So it would. What a trial I am to you, Geoffrey. I'm really sorry," said Antony, unrepentant. "And as for what we'll say ot Messrs. Kirby, Shields, and Connolly, I haven't the faintest idea at the moment, but I'm sure between us we'll think of something."

"I'm sure we shall, no matter how unconvincing," said Geoffrey, declining to be comforted. "How long do you propose to devote to this operation? It seems to me to be nothing but a waste of time."

"Tomorrow is also a good day."

"Tomorrow's Saturday," Geoffrey expostulated. "Besides, we can't possibly—"

"If you don't want to come along—"

"I didn't say that. I suppose you're going to tell me we ought to devote both Saturday and Sunday to this singularly profitless cause."

"We shall both be busy once the courts open," Maitland pointed out. "Come on, Geoffrey, one weekend's work won't hurt you," he added persuasively. And then, more practically, "You'll feel better when you've had your lunch."

He told Jenny all about it over dinner. It had taken him a long time, longer than it should have done, but at last he had learned that anything at all was preferable to her to being kept in the dark. "And I know you're not happy about it," he said when he had finished – they were sitting by the fire with their coffee by then – "any more than Geoffrey is. But honestly, love, what do you think is going to happen?"

"You believe that these enquiries may lead you to the organiser of the art thefts, don't you?" asked Jenny flatly. She wasn't in a mood to wrap things up.

"Not necessarily. Louise Chorley must have had a very wide acquaintance. I'm interested in these people purely and simply because they seem to be the only ones with the necessary knowledge to have framed Alan Kirby."

"If he was framed," said Jenny.

"Come now, love, it's not like you to be thinking the worst of anybody."

"When a crime has been committed, somebody has to be guilty," Jenny pointed out with unaccustomed logic. "So if I exonerate Alan Kirby in my own mind I've got to think badly about somebody else."

"That's true. Anyway, you're so far right, love, I do feel a special interest in Daniel Kirby, because he's just the sort

32

of person Julian Verlaine – you remember him? Emily Walpole's partner – thought the organiser of these thefts must be. Someone who knows art, and knows other collectors. But that's not to say I'm right about him. Alan Kirby is really my only concern."

"You'd better tell that to Uncle Nick," said Jenny sceptically.

"Uncle Nick? I wasn't proposing to tell him anything at all." Maitland might have seen daylight where his wife was concerned, but he still laboured under the delusion – in spite of a good deal of proof to the contrary – that it was possible to keep things from Sir Nicholas.

"Antony, you know we've had lunch with him every Saturday for years and years and years, he and Vera will be expecting us tomorrow. You've outlined a pretty heavy day's activities, and I don't suppose for a moment you'll be there, so what am I to say to him?"

"Just that Geoffrey and I are looking into a very minor matter. We have a client accused of receiving stolen goods, and have some reason to think he may not be guilty after all."

"I suppose I must," said Jenny. And then, more cheerfully, "It doesn't sound very serious, receiving stolen goods. Not compared with some of the things you've been mixed up in, I mean."

"Serious enough to young Kirby," Antony reminded her. "But as for the rest, forget it! It's all quite straightforward."

They had arranged to meet outside Mrs Campbell's boarding-house in Earls Court at ten o'clock the following morning, and take their chance about whom they found at home. In the meantime Geoffrey would have done some telephoning concerning possible interviews the following day, and the first thing he did when Antony arrived was to tell him that he had had some good fortune there, and everything was arranged.

"Weren't any of them going to be away for the weekend?" queried Maitland, rather surprised.

"Not one. And that was queer, Antony, they might each of them have been expecting me to get in touch with them."

"No awkward questions?" said Antony, with the amusement back in his voice.

"Not one."

"Well, perhaps it's a good omen. Let's punch the bell, and see if we have as much luck here."

The door was opened to them by a scrawny little girl in a neat print frock, and with a chronically scared expression. "We haven't any rooms vacant," she blurted out before either of them could speak. "I suppose you'd be wanting something right away, because Aunt says there might be something next month."

Antony and Geoffrey exchanged glances, the same thought in both their minds. Mrs Campbell was expecting to lose a lodger, when Alan Kirby was sent to prison.

"That isn't our present errand," Geoffrey explained. "Looking for rooms, I mean, though I'm sure you make everybody very comfortable here." It was a well-kept house compared with some of the others in the street, but it did occur to Antony that it must have been something of a comedown for their client after his uncle's home.

"What would you be wanting then? Aunt never buys at the door."

"No, we're not selling anything either. Is Mrs Campbell

34

in? We should very much like to see her if she is, and perhaps if she permits us to ask you a few questions too."

That last was a mistake, the scared look intensified. "Aunt is here," she admitted, "but *I* don't know anything you could possibly want to hear about. Besides I have to be getting on with my work."

"Nothing at all to worry you," said Geoffrey soothingly. "And I don't suppose for a moment that a well-organised young lady like yourself has any chores left at this hour on Saturday morning. But perhaps if you tell Mrs Campbell we're here, and give her my card, she'll agree to see us."

The card was almost snatched from him, and the door shut in their faces. They did not, however, have long to wait before it opened again. "She'll see you," said the girl breathlessly, "and I can stay and listen if I like." This last was said a little defiantly, as though she had expected that permission would be refused, but perhaps her aunt's acceptance of the visitors had calmed her fears a little.

"That's a very good idea," said Horton cordially. "There may be some points upon which you can put us straight."

"If it's about our Mr Kirby, which is what Aunt said it must be when she read your card, I don't know anything about him at all. Aunt is strict about that, no mixing with our guests." She was preceding them down the hall as she spoke, and their first impression of the house was confirmed. Everything, including the linoleum, was polished until it shone. And there was no smell of cabbage (which Antony had always understood was mandatory in a lodging-house), only of the rather pleasant polish that had been used. The girl threw open a door at the back of the hall. "Here they are, Aunt," she announced.

It was more of a sitting-room than the kitchen Antony had been expecting, with an open fire – though the season was still too warm for it to be needed – several comfortable chairs, and a Welsh dresser that looked as if it might be a genuine antique. If the room had ever contained stove and sink, they had long since been banished to the scullery, along with any necessary, more modern appurtenances. Mrs Campbell was a chunky little woman, with grey hair combed straight back from a red, shiny face. She had got

35

up to greet them, and he was surprised to notice how easily she moved, considering Kirby's reference to arthritis. But then he noticed her hands; that was where the trouble lay, they were gnarled and twisted with the disease. This didn't seem to cause her any embarrassment, for she insisted on shaking hands with each of the visitors, and then invited them quite cordially to seat themselves.

"And the young lady?" said Geoffrey, obeying her. "Your niece, I believe."

"My husband's niece," she corrected him. "Nancy Campbell. She doesn't have anything to do with our guests, but she can stay if she likes."

"It isn't a question of knowing about your boarders," Geoffrey explained. "We want to find out if anybody strange has been seen entering the house."

"I thought it was about our Mr Kirby."

"Yes, it is in a way, we're his lawyers. But, you see, if he didn't put the painting in his wardrobe, somebody else did."

"But he's been arrested," she said, as though that closed the matter. "Stop fidgeting, Nancy, and sit still."

"That doesn't quite end the matter," Geoffrey told her. "There's still the trial to come, and that's where we come in." Considering his opinion about his client, Geoffrey was doing pretty well, Antony thought.

"Well now, I never thought of that. But nobody comes into this house without my knowing it, except it was by accident. And they couldn't rely on that," she added, shrewdly enough.

"But I understand you were away the weekend before the painting was found. Mr Kirby says it wasn't in his room on the Friday evening, and he was in himself until after tea on Saturday. So there's Saturday evening, most of Sunday, and Monday while he was at work to account for."

"I was only away the one night," she said thoughtfully, "and back by ten o'clock on the Sunday. But Nancy locked the door like I told her, I had to let myself in with my key. And I'm pretty sure, though it's not something I could take me oath on, that nobody strange came in all day Monday."

36

"Perhaps somebody known to you, then?" Antony suggested.

"Well, of course, that's different. There was Mrs Kirby of course, I've seen her often enough visiting her nephew."

"Mrs Hilda Kirby?" Maitland had taken over now.

"Aunt Hilda he calls her. She said she'd been having tea with him, I think it was on the Saturday, and he'd taken so much trouble to get the things she liked she wanted to show him she was grateful. So she brought him a cake."

"Did you see her arrive, Mrs Campbell?"

"No, that's funny, I didn't. She was coming downstairs and stopped to have a word with me. A nice lady she is, no side about her at all."

"Her husband wasn't with her?"

"No, not on that occasion. Not often, in fact."

"Any other visitors, then?"

"Not that day. Not to my knowledge."

"And you think you'd have seen them if there had been?"

"Going or coming, I'm pretty sure of that. I like to know what's going on in me own house," she added unnecessarily.

"That leaves us with Sunday, then, as the most likely time. What about you, Miss Campbell?" he said, turning and smiling at the girl. "Were you in all that day?"

"Yes, of course I was. Aunt says it wouldn't do for us both to be out together."

"Then perhaps you can tell us what you saw."

"Nothing at all," she answered. She thought about that for a moment and then evidently felt it needed some amplification. "I'm not particularly interested," she said, rather grandly.

"She means she's not nosy like I am." Mrs Campbell gave a surprisingly jolly laugh. "All the same, my girl, you must have seen something."

"Well, I didn't then."

"Try to think," Antony urged her. "What did you do all day? I know you must be busy with a big place like this to look after, but I expect you try to get most of your chores done during the week, don't you?"

"We don't do meals at weekends," said Mrs Campbell flatly. "And Nancy has plenty of time to herself, she can't say otherwise. There was just that night I wanted to visit my sister, so she had to stay in the house while I was away."

"You stayed in your own quarters here all day on the Sunday?"

"Well, I wouldn't say that," said Nancy reluctantly. "I was upstairs a few times, our bedrooms are up there you know, on the top floor, and there's a little sitting-room when Aunt wants to entertain."

"And on these excursions, you saw nothing?"

"Only Mr Ramsey and Miss Gardiner. They went out together about half-past ten in the morning I should say."

"You didn't see Mr Kirby at all?"

"Not that day. All was so quiet, I thought he must have gone out really early, he'd have been playing his records otherwise."

"And you saw nobody else all day?"

"Mr Brewster, of course."

"He's one of your ... tenants?"

"Yes, the oldest of them in more senses than one." Mrs Campbell took it upon herself to reply. "He has the big room that used to be the drawing-room, it's opposite the dining-room so it's easy for him, and there's a cloakroom on this floor so he doesn't have to tackle the stairs, only for a bath once a week."

"He *can* manage them then?"

"It's a difficult job, but he can when he wants."

"Might he have seen something, do you think?"

"He sits in the window a lot, he could have done easily. But don't be getting your hopes up, the police have talked to him as they've talked to the rest of us. He had nothing to tell them."

"We'd still very much like to see him," Antony assured her. "But Nancy was going to tell us about seeing him that Sunday."

"No mystery about that, I went in to make sure he had something to eat," said Nancy. "He takes his meals with the rest of them weekdays, but sometimes on Saturday and

38

Sunday he's just too tired to bother to get anything for himself."

"Was he tired that day?"

"Not particularly. He'd warmed up some soup for his lunch, and said he had some cold ham that would do for dinner. So I came back here, and got on with me book. It's not often I've time to have a good read. And that's something I like doing."

"Then there's only one more question, and I want an answer from you both. Do you know the size of the roll of canvas that was found in Mr Kirby's wardrobe?"

"Police showed it to me, wanted to know if I'd seen him bringing it in."

"And had you?"

"No, I hadn't."

"Wasn't that rather odd, as you say you like to know what's going on in the house?"

"That doesn't include watching our guests come home from work," said Mrs Campbell. "I know to a minute when he comes in, so if I hear anything then I don't bother."

"I see. Does the same thing go for you, Nancy?"

"I never saw him with anything like that."

"Then have you seen such a thing in anybody else's possession? Either of you?" he added hopefully, looking from one of them to the other.

Nancy contented herself with shaking her head. Mrs Campbell said, "No," quite positively. "And if I had," she went on, "do you think I wouldn't have told them?"

"You mean the police?"

"Of course I do."

"You like Mr Alan Kirby, don't you?"

"I don't know how you made that out, but I do. Only I've seen enough of this world to know a man can be very likeable and still be a bad lot."

"Does he have many visitors?"

"Only his aunt as a regular thing, and his uncle sometimes. But he and Miss Gardiner and Mr Ramsey are in and out of each other's rooms all the time."

"Then perhaps they may have seen something. Will you do something for me, Nancy? See if Mr Brewster is up, and if he's well enough to see us."

39

She grinned at him surprisingly, and all of a sudden the awe in which she obviously held her aunt seemed to be dissipated. "He'll feel well enough," she assured him. "As nosy as Aunt Dolly is, that's Mr Brewster."

She darted out into the hall as she spoke, and Antony and Geoffrey remained behind to make their farewells, rather expecting a thunderbolt. However, Mrs Campbell seemed rather pleased than otherwise by this unexpected show of spirit. "I'll make something of that girl yet," she assured them. And if neither of them thought her generally impressive manner was the best way to go about this they naturally kept the idea to themselves.

Out in the gleaming hall Nancy was waiting for them. "He'll see you," she whispered excitedly. And then, still confidentially, "Don't be too disappointed by what Aunt said about him not knowing anything to tell the police. He has his good days and his bad ones."

"You mean that some days he might remember something that another day he'd forget?"

"Yes, that's right. I'd say today is one of the good days. And take your time, he'll enjoy having visitors."

"You don't think we'll tire him?"

"I don't think it matters," said Nancy bluntly. Antony was pondering the exact meaning of this remark as he followed Geoffrey into Mr Brewster's room.

If Alan Kirby's estimate of his neighbour's age had been an exaggeration, Antony felt that it wasn't too unreasonable. Mr Brewster was certainly a very old man. He was sitting near the window, and didn't attempt to get up, and his face under a shock of white hair was already so wrinkled that it was difficult to tell whether he was smiling or not. But his voice was cordial and he waved aside Geoffrey's apologies quite airily. It seemed likely that Nancy's idea that he would be pleased to have someone to talk to had been pretty near the mark.

"Come in," he said, "come in both of you and sit down." His voice was cracked and quavering, but quite strong for all that. "What's all this that girl tells me? You're acting for that young rascal Alan Kirby? Do you think he deserves your help?"

40

Geoffrey was starting, "Everyone is entitled to representation – " when Antony interrupted him.

"As a matter of fact," he said firmly, "I do."

"Well now, well, that's a new idea to me. Mrs Campbell told me what happened. Of course that wasn't exactly gossip, I asked her, because I'd seen the police coming here several times."

"Do you know Alan Kirby, Mr Brewster?"

"See him at breakfast most days. I'm not one for lying in bed. Dinner too sometimes. Though these young things, they're always on the move."

"What do you think of him then?"

"Nice enough young chap."

"You sounded as though... you seem to be taking his guilt for granted."

"In my day," said Mr Brewster, rather grandly, "the police didn't make mistakes."

Geoffrey said rather quickly, because he felt it likely that Maitland would want to argue the point, "You're well placed here for seeing any comings and goings. That's really why we'd like your help."

"Yes, and I take an interest in things too, which is more than I can say for some people. And that girl, Nancy, she keeps me up to date with what's going on."

"I dare say most days," said Antony, taking up the questioning again, "you see the other boarders coming home from work?"

"Don't let Mrs Campbell hear you say that," said the old man with a cackle of amusement. "Paying guests, that's what we are. But yes, you're quite right, I do see them; not that there's much interest in that."

"You know what Alan Kirby is charged with, don't you?"

"It seems someone told me. Said he stole a painting, something like that."

"The charge is receiving stolen goods," said Geoffrey, anxious, as always, to get the record straight. "The painting concerned was stolen at the beginning of June, and we're wondering how it got into the house."

For the first time a rather vague look came over the old man's face. "I have a sort of idea," he said, "that someone

41

else asked me something like that, not too long ago. It would have been in a crate, no doubt, not an easy thing to hide. But I don't quite remember—"

"The painting had been taken from its frame," Antony took up the explanation. "It was a large canvas" – he measured with his hands, knowing well enough that Geoffrey had the exact measurements on the tip of his tongue, but feeling that they would confuse Mr Brewster – "and when it was discovered at the back of Mr Kirby's wardrobe it was rolled up. But even in that form, out of its frame, it wouldn't be easy to hide. Not the sort of thing you could put under your jacket, for instance."

"Alan Kirby always carries a briefcase," the old man volunteered.

"I'm afraid that wouldn't be big enough either. You've never seen him with such a thing under his arm?"

"What sort of a question is that? I thought you were on his side."

"I am," Antony explained. "It isn't easy to prove a negative, but at least it would be helpful to know that you *didn't* see him with any such burden."

"Well, I didn't. Nor either of those other young things, friends of his."

"People who visited him?"

"No, the two that live here. Jackie and Bernard, I can't be bothered remembering their other names."

"I know you've been over all this with the police before, but—"

"Nothing of the sort. They haven't been near me."

That took Antony aback for a moment; perhaps the good day that Nancy had mentioned was already a thing of the past. "Mrs Campbell says that Alan Kirby didn't have many visitors," he ventured after a moment.

"Sort of thing she'd know," said Mr Brewster. "I see who comes to the house, of course, but if you want the truth" – confidentially – "I do drop off sometimes. Only of course I wouldn't know who they were visiting . . . the people I see, I mean."

"No, of course not."

Mr Brewster was looking from one to the other of them

in a puzzled way. "You did tell me why you wanted to see me," he said doubtfully.

"Yes, indeed we did," said Geoffrey. "You remember the police coming, and then hearing that Alan Kirby had been arrested. We're his lawyers."

"Of course I remember that. I don't understand what you want with me though."

It was only too obvious that he had already completely forgotten the conversation they had just had. "We're interested in knowing," said Geoffrey carefully, "whether you've ever seen anyone coming to the house with a roll of canvas about this long" – he imitated Antony in measuring with his hands – "at the beginning of September, most likely on Sunday the third."

"I can't tell you when, but I certainly saw him," said the old man. "Not the sort of thing you could miss."

"Saw whom?" Antony was too eager, and saw at once that this had been a mistake. "Was it someone you knew, Mr Brewster?" he asked carefully.

"No one I knew, but it seems I've seen him before."

"A regular visitor?"

"No, I wouldn't say that. It was this roll – paper I thought it was – that caught my eye. But it does seem to me I'd seen him some time before."

"Could you describe the man?"

"A medium looking sort of chap."

"Tall?" The old man shook his head. "Well, was he fat or thin, can you tell me what colour his hair was?"

"Medium, I said. And he was wearing a hat, and a light raincoat. It was drizzling that afternoon," said Mr Brewster, suddenly apparently quite clear-headed.

"But you don't remember the date?"

"No, I don't. But it must have been a weekend because I'd just seen Alan Kirby go out, not five minutes before. And he wouldn't have been going out in the middle of a weekday afternoon."

"Have you any idea about the time?"

"I'd finished my lunch and that girl Nancy had been to see if I'd managed something. I dare say it was half an hour after she left me, might have been two o'clock or half past."

43

And that, though they tried in turns for another half hour, was as far as they could get. When they were out into the gleaming hall again with the door tight shut behind them Antony and Geoffrey exchanged a hopeless look. "He wouldn't be the faintest use as a witness," said Maitland gloomily.

"I shouldn't worry too much about that," Horton consoled him. "It seems he had no recollection at all of this when the police spoke to him, but even if he'd told them the story, even if he repeated it in court quite clearly and was believed, the man he saw might just as well have been bringing the canvas to Alan Kirby by arrangement."

"So he might. And we haven't the faintest idea," Antony added with a glimmer of humour, "whether he was telling the truth to us or to the police. He may have imagined the whole thing."

"Well, there's one thing we *can* do," said Geoffrey, suddenly brisk. "If Kirby's in, we can ask him what sort of a day it was that Sunday. You were still away, and I can't for the life of me remember, but subsequent events may have etched the whole thing more clearly in his mind."

At this point the door at the back of the hall opened and Mrs Campbell appeared. "Have you finished then?" she asked.

"With Mr Brewster, yes."

"Haven't upset him, have you?"

"No, I don't think so. You may find he's a little confused about why we visited him."

"Yes, I could have told you it would be a waste of time. What else do you want?"

"Do you know if Mr Kirby is in?"

"I'm pretty sure he is."

"And your two other paying guests?"

"I haven't heard any of them go out."

"Then may we go up? Or do you prefer to announce visitors?"

"I do not. If you think I've time for larks like that you're mistaken. Go straight upstairs and you'll find Mr Kirby's door on your left when you turn on to the landing. He'll tell you where the others are."

"Thank you, Mrs Campbell, thank you very much

44

indeed for your help." Antony was already half way up the stairs, and Geoffrey, his sense of propriety satisfied, made haste to follow him. A tap on the door that Mrs Campbell had indicated brought a summons in Alan Kirby's voice to enter. Maitland stood aside to let his instructing solicitor go in first.

Kirby was writing at a table near the window, but he scrambled to his feet when he saw them. "I thought it was Jackie and Bernard," he said. "I didn't expect to see you again so soon, either of you."

"I think you knew we should be making some enquiries," said Antony. "This was the natural place to start. And out of our talk with Mr Brewster, one or two things have arisen."

"Mr Brewster? He sits at the window all day, and probably sees everything that goes on. But sometimes he remembers and sometimes he doesn't. I think the police had already questioned him."

"So I understand. We realise well enough we can't use his evidence, he seemed to have a lucid interval today but that might not occur again at the right moment. However, it would be helpful to be able to confirm, for our own guidance, whether the story he told us was likely to be true or not. I don't mean that he was lying—"

"No, he gets muddled," said Alan indulgently. "What did he tell you?"

Maitland didn't answer that directly. "Do you remember what the weather was like on Sunday the third of September?" he asked.

"Two days before the police came? Yes, as it happens I do. It was drizzling most of the day."

"You said you were in and out of the house, do you remember any more than that?"

"I went to church in the morning. I realise that isn't exactly the fashionable thing to do," he added defensively, "but I got into the habit when I was living with Aunt Hilda."

"No need to apologise." Maitland was amused again. "Did you come home after that?"

"Yes, I came in for lunch, but I wasn't here very long. I remember because Jackie and Bernard had asked me to

45

join them. We often used to lunch together at the weekend, but I had a feeling that day that a third person wasn't wanted, and it turned out I was quite right, they got engaged."

"You say you weren't in for long," said Maitland, ignoring this interesting piece of information.

"No, I suppose I went out again about two o'clock."

"Did you see anybody you knew?"

"There weren't many people about, it was a miserable day. Why are you asking me all this?"

"Because Mr Brewster thinks he saw somebody come into the house with a large canvas under his arm just after you went out that day. I may tell you that what you have said confirms his story as to time and the kind of weather it was, but, as you said, and as had already occurred to us, his evidence would be worse than useless in court."

"That's a pity, isn't it? Still, it's a beginning," said Kirby, who was evidently something of an optimist.

"Yes, as you say. Mrs Campbell seems to think that your friends Miss Gardiner and Mr Ramsey are also at home."

Alan glanced at his watch. "I think they are, but you'd better hurry if you want to catch them. They usually go out to lunch about this time."

Antony got to his feet. "Are you still being tactful?" he asked, smiling.

"No, it's this article I'm writing. I want to get it finished, so I'll just have a glass of beer and a sandwich." He glanced in a rather puzzled way at Geoffrey Horton, who, except for the first greetings, had been silent throughout the interview. "If Mr Brewster really did see this man," he said doubtfully, "perhaps someone else might have done so too. Someone in one of the other houses."

"I shall have enquiries put in hand, of course," said Geoffrey. "You can be sure of that." He didn't add the opinion he had already expressed to Maitland, that any evidence on the point would be worse than useless, as the painting might have been delivered by arrangement.

Out on the landing, Horton tapped on the nearest door. There was no reply, but a moment later one of the other doors burst open and a willowy dark girl dressed in the height of fashion erupted on to the landing. She was closely

46

followed by a young man of about her own age and very little taller. "Let's see if we can rout Alan out after all," he was saying, but broke off when he saw the two strangers.

"I think perhaps you must be Miss Gardiner and Mr Ramsey," said Horton.

"Yes, we are." It was the girl who answered him. "You've just come from Alan's room, haven't you? Are you friends of his?"

"I think you may say that in a way we are," said Geoffrey. "We're his lawyers." He went on to introduce Maitland, and to express their desire for some conversation.

Ramsey was looking at Antony with interest. "I've heard of you, Mr Maitland," he said, and Geoffrey saw his friend stiffen. "Look here," – Bernard turned impulsively to the girl – "we were just going out to lunch. Why don't we ask them to join us?"

"Is the idea for you to pump us or for us to pump you?" said Antony, recovering himself quickly.

"Both, I suppose," said Ramsey cheerfully. "What do you say, Jackie?"

"I think it's a wizard idea."

"Then that's what we'll do, but I think we must insist that you lunch with us. Is that all right with you, Geoffrey?" Antony asked.

"It certainly is. As you know the district, Mr Ramsey–"

"Yes, there's a place just round the corner. If you have a car parked I'd leave it where it is, it isn't always so easy to find a new spot."

As they made their way down the street Antony found himself walking beside Jacqueline Gardiner. "Did Alan tell you I'm going to be Mrs Ramsey soon?" she asked him.

"Yes, he did. I should have offered you my felicitations," said Antony formally. And then he smiled at her. "Something tells me Mr Ramsey isn't going to find life dull."

"Well, I should hope not," said Jackie, with mock severity. "What about these questions of yours?"

"They'll wait until we've found a table and given our order," said Maitland. "And you needn't be expecting

47

fireworks, because I think it will be rather a dull session."
But privately he was thinking that that was one thing that
anyone in Jacqueline Gardiner's presence would never
be.

Sir Nicholas and Lady Harding were already enjoying a
quiet pre-luncheon sherry when Jenny came downstairs to
join them. The study was Sir Nicholas's favourite room,
and they used it for all but the most formal gatherings.
Jenny, who held them both in a great deal of affection,
paused in the doorway to observe them for a moment,
before she herself was seen. Sir Nicholas was stretched out
in his chair, completely at his ease; a man with an air of
unconscious authority about him, as tall as his nephew but
much more heavily built. He had always been very fair, so
that the white hairs that mingled with the others now
were scarcely visible, and he was good-looking enough to
be generally referred to as handsome by the newspapers; on
which occasions Jenny in the past, and now Vera, made it
a rule to sequester the offending edition. His temper was
never of the most equable, and certainly not equal to
withstanding a comment like that.

His wife, Vera, was a tall woman, with a great deal of
greying hair that was always escaping from confinement,
rather like the White Queen's. She had a gruff, rather
elliptical way of speaking, and a preference for sack-like
garments; though since her marriage she seemed to have
discovered a sense of colour, and the sacks were now well
cut. She smiled at Jenny when she realised she was
standing in the doorway, and Sir Nicholas came to his feet
with an immediate offer of refreshment. He was half way
across the room when he paused.

"Antony isn't with you?" he said.

"No, Uncle Nick, he sent his apologies to you both. He
had to work."

Vera stretched out a welcoming hand. "Come and sit
down, Jenny," she invited. "That was bad luck, with the
session not even begun."

"Yes, it was. He was very sorry." Jenny was the worst
person in the world to be asked to prevaricate, particularly
to people of whom she was fond. But Antony – however

48

unreasonably – wanted to avoid any explanation at the moment, and she'd do what she could to deal with the situation as he wished.

"I don't remember hearing of any conference arranged in chambers for this morning," said Sir Nicholas, coming back across the room with a glass of the very dry sherry that he and Vera preferred, and that Jenny, too, had got used to since her marriage. "In any case, why arrange it for lunch time?"

"It wasn't exactly that, Uncle Nick, I mean, it wasn't in chambers. He had to see somebody . . . Geoffrey's with him," she stressed.

"Am I supposed to be grateful for that?" asked Sir Nicholas, seating himself again. "Now which of his clients, I wonder, has affairs that call for so much overtime?"

"Quite a simple case, Uncle Nick. Nothing complicated at all." Jenny was quite well aware that she was saying too much and pulled herself up sharply. "A man accused of receiving stolen goods."

"Geoffrey, I presume, is convinced of the man's innocence."

"I don't know what Geoffrey thinks." But Jenny was, at any time, a transparent person, and her discomfort was only too obvious.

"It would be more to the point perhaps to ask what *sort* of stolen goods," said Sir Nicholas, laying his finger neatly on the one point she wished to avoid.

"A painting," said Jenny reluctantly.

"That covers rather a wide field. Perhaps you can be more exact, my dear."

"A Rubens," said Jenny. "It was stolen from the Sefton Gallery, but Antony's client isn't accused of that. Only of receiving it."

"That makes a difference, of course," said Sir Nicholas gravely. But he exchanged a glance with Vera, and in both of their looks there was something uneasy. They were remembering a conversation they had had together, some six months before, when they had heard, through the indiscretion of a journalist who considered himself indebted to Antony, of the story Louise Chorley had given to

49

his newspaper. "I take it," Sir Nicholas went on, "that Antony feels there is some case for further investigation... I seem to have heard him use that phrase before. But even he must have had some reason for that opinion."

"Don't tease the child," said Vera gruffly. "Obvious enough she doesn't want to tell you—"

"It isn't that," said Jenny, with a disregard for the truth that was completely uncharacteristic, and also completely obvious. "But there is one funny thing, Uncle Nick," she added, hoping that the explanation would satisfy him. "The police went to this Mr Kirby's lodgings because of an anonymous telephone call."

"When thieves fall out," said Sir Nicholas, and shrugged.

"You don't think—?"

"I don't think Antony had any idea in his mind, when I spoke to him last, of undertaking an investigation into any of the cases on his current list," said Sir Nicholas flatly. "You may as well tell me, Jenny, because I shall certainly ask him as soon as he comes home. What is he doing that he'd rather Vera and I didn't know about?"

Jenny cast an anguished glance at Vera. "It all started with Kevin O'Brien's visit the other evening," she said.

"What has Kevin O'Brien to do with this client of Antony's?"

"Nothing at all." Jenny was not noted for the lucidity of her explanations.

"Well then."

"You remember Louise Chorley?" said Jenny desperately.

"Of course I remember her. Don't tell me—"

"Kevin's defending her," Jenny told him.

"Good God!" said Sir Nicholas, and was momentarily silenced.

"When she heard about Alan Kirby, she said he couldn't possibly have done such a thing," said Jenny, taking heart. "So Antony thought he'd better see him."

"That seems rather flimsy grounds, even for him."

"I do wish you wouldn't keep saying 'even for him', Uncle Nick," said Jenny, quite crossly.

50

"I dare say Antony didn't mean to take it any further," said Vera pacifically. "What happened, Jenny, when he and Geoffrey talked to their client?"

"He said he wasn't guilty," said Jenny, shying away from any further description of the conference. "And I think Antony believed him. It's all quite reasonable, Uncle Nick, he'll make what enquiries he can and then stop."

For a long moment Sir Nicholas looked at her in silence. "Do you remember the motive Louise Chorley gave *The Courier* for the shooting of her husband?" he asked.

"Of course I do."

Sir Nicholas turned to his wife. "And do you remember, my dear, the conversation we had the evening we first heard of it? We said we wondered how this man, this lover of Louise Chorley's who was apparently organising the art thefts, would feel about Antony's part in the affair."

"Talk about it later," said Vera, her eyes on Jenny's face.

"You needn't worry about me," said Jenny. "I've already pointed all that out to Antony, and so, I think, has Geoffrey."

"Pointed what out?"

"That he should have avoided being actively concerned in any case concerning art thefts at the moment," said Jenny, with unaccustomed clarity, "but the fact that Louise Chorley is tied up in it somehow makes matters worse."

"Let's think about it." If Sir Nicholas was gratified by Jenny's apparent grasp of the situation, he didn't show it. "Mrs Chorley must have known Antony's client—"

"And *he* knew *her*. She was a friend of his aunt's. He used to live with Daniel Kirby and his wife until he came down from university."

"Is that Daniel Kirby the collector?"

"I'm afraid it is," said Jenny in a small voice.

"Worse and worse!" Sir Nicholas, however, sounded more resigned than anything else. Then he added, seeing Jenny's stricken look, "Don't worry yourself, child. Almost certainly it's nothing but a coincidence. The mere fact that they know each other—"

"Alan Kirby told Antony there were three people who

51

knew where his room is in the boarding-house he lives in,"
said Jenny. "His landlady doesn't encourage visitors. Well,
four people really, but I don't suppose his aunt had
anything to do with it. I think Antony suspects Daniel
Kirby of being this organiser they talk about. Though he
can't understand, in that case, why he should have planted
the painting on his nephew. For one thing it was very
valuable."

"Antony has been wrong before, so we'll hope he is again
this time," said Sir Nicholas. And then, not altogether
consistently, "Did you do nothing to dissuade him,
Jenny?"

"You know I never do," said Jenny simply.

"Don't you?"

Vera divided one of her rather grim smiles between
them. "Take a man to be so blind," she said. "*You*'ve tried
to dissuade him, Nicholas, but have you ever succeeded?"

"I can't remember any such occasion," Sir Nicholas
admitted.

"And you'd have thought the worse of him if you had,"
Vera insisted.

At that her husband smiled at her. "I suppose I should,"
he conceded. "Would you rather I didn't mention this
business to him, Jenny?"

"No, I don't think so," she said slowly. "I don't think I'm
very good at keeping secrets, look at the way I've told you
everything now. So Antony's bound to find out that you
know."

"And that I've heard a much clearer story under
cross-examination than if you'd set out to give us a
statement of the facts," said Sir Nicholas, smiling at her.
"You haven't touched your sherry, Jenny, and you look as
if it would do you good. You mustn't worry your head over
Antony, most likely he'll come to his senses before the
weekend's out."

"Any case, nothing to be done," said Vera. "Who is this
Daniel Kirby, Nicholas?"

From answering that question, Sir Nicholas gradually
led the conversation away from the subject of his nephew's
vagaries. By the time luncheon was over Jenny had

52

recovered her spirits, at least as far as appearances went, but though Sir Nicholas was deceived by this to a certain extent, the same cannot be said for his wife.

The restaurant to which Jacqueline Gardiner and Bernard Ramsey took their companions was almost aggressively clean, but that was about all that could be said in its favour. Antony was surprised to find that it was open at weekends, because it was practically empty. Obviously its busy time was during the week, at least he hoped it was, or there would be bankruptcy proceedings in train before the proprietor was very much older. Jacqueline led the way to a table in the corner. "This is nice, isn't it?" she said, seating herself and beaming round at them. "We've both talked to the police, of course, but this is much more fun."

"I don't know that I should exactly call it fun," said Bernard a little repressively. "Alan is in a damn difficult position, but if these gentlemen can do something to get him out of it—"

"We shall do our best," said Geoffrey, and saw without surprise Maitland's quick frown at the use of the phrase, which was one he particularly disliked. But if the solicitor meant to go on he didn't get the chance because Antony interrupted him.

"You're friends of Alan Kirby's," he said. "What do you think of him?"

"He's a good chap, he wouldn't do anything dishonest," said Bernard shortly.

"And you, Miss Gardiner?"

"I'm mad about him," said Jacqueline. "No, you needn't scowl, Bernard, I like him, I don't love him. And if he really did steal the painting I should still like him," she added defiantly.

"The charge is one of receiving stolen goods," said Geoffrey, with his passion for accuracy.

"Yes, I know, but it means the same thing, doesn't it?"

"Not at all the same thing."

"It means he knew that it was stolen and that would be just as bad."

53

"Wait a bit, Jackie," Bernard protested. "You know Alan says he's innocent. And I, for one, believe him."

"Yes, but he'd be bound to say that wouldn't he?" she appealed to the others. "Mind you, it'd be difficult to get the thing into the house without our gorgon of a landlady seeing him, but I understand he had three months to do it in after all."

"That difficulty would apply to anybody, but there was one weekend when Mrs Campbell was away."

"I thought all of you were cynics," said Jackie smiling at him. "But here you are, believing everything you're told."

"Oh, I think we are, terrible cynics." He broke off as a waitress approached and waited until she had left again with their orders. "Before we start won't you tell us a little about yourselves?" he invited when they were alone.

It was Ramsey who took it upon himself to reply. "Jackie's a model," he told them. "I suppose you might have guessed that from her figure, and the way she wears her clothes, and all that goo she puts on her face."

"Would you have done?" Jacqueline demanded.

"If you want the truth, Miss Gardiner," said Antony seriously, "I thought the members of your profession had to be a little more – a little more statuesque. Not quite so lively."

"Oh, we do. It's one of the things I find most difficult, but of course it's only just as long as you're actually modelling. And since Bernard told you about me I'll tell you about him. He's a chartered accountant, and he's got a job in the City which is going to lead to great things."

To which, thought Antony to himself, there is no reply. "How long have you both known Alan Kirby?" he said aloud.

"He was already at Mrs Campbell's when I went there about two years ago," said Bernard. "We hit it off right away, and saw a good deal of each other."

"And then I came along about six months later," said Jackie, "and threw a spanner in the works, if I may put it that way."

"Now what exactly do you mean by that?"

"Well, for a little while they both wanted to take me

54

out," she said confidingly. "Then Alan sort of fell out of the race, and of course Bernard hadn't quite as much time for him as he'd had before."

"If you think Alan cared about that you're wrong," said Bernard firmly. "He was far more interested in those articles he was writing for *The Courier*. Dull stuff, if you ask me, but he found it fascinating."

"You know something about his tastes, I suppose. Has he any interest in art?"

"You wouldn't need to be interested in a thing to steal it for profit," said Jackie. Bernard silenced her with a look. As for Antony, he had long since decided that freedom from dullness wasn't everything, there was a good deal to be said for a quiet life.

"I don't think he had any interest at all," Ramsey said. "Not in art in general or paintings in particular. Books were his thing, books and music. Though of course you know that his uncle is a great name in the art world?"

"Yes, I'd heard that. Just as a matter of interest, Mr Ramsey, how did you come to have heard of me?"

"I read the newspapers," said Ramsey, rather too bluntly for his interrogator's taste. Publicity, in Antony's experience, need not necessarily be friendly.

"Does Kirby have many visitors?" he asked by way of changing the subject.

"Very few indeed. Mrs Campbell is strict about that. I don't just mean he couldn't entertain a young lady in his rooms, she discourages visitors in general. So there was just his aunt, not the most lively of companions but I think he's fond of her. And a couple of times he mentioned that his uncle had come along as well. Otherwise I don't remember anybody at all."

"So if any plotting was done, Miss Gardiner, it was done elsewhere," said Antony with a smile. "You spoke about the difficulty of introducing the rolled up canvas to his room. Have you any idea how that could have been done?"

"It would have been easier for us than for anybody else," said Bernard, a little ruefully. "Mrs Campbell doesn't bother to rush to the kitchen door every time we come in, I mean she knows our times pretty well."

"That rather contradicts what you said before. Kirby could have taken it in himself equally easily."

"Yes, I suppose so."

"You've never seen anything that could help us in this connection?"

"I'm afraid not."

"And that's what you told the police?"

"Yes, of course it is," they said, practically in chorus. And Jacqueline added, "I wouldn't have told them anyway, even if I'd seen Alan with it under his arm."

"But you didn't?"

"No, I didn't."

"We've been talking to Mr Brewster this morning."

"Oh him, he's practically gaga," said Jacqueline scornfully. "What on earth good could that do?"

"No good at all, unfortunately. He claims to have seen somebody – on a day that could have been the Sunday Mrs Campbell was away – enter the house with a rolled up canvas."

"That wasn't what he told the police."

"No, I realise that. He may have forgotten it at that time, or he may have imagined the whole thing when he was talking to us this morning. There's just no telling. Do you – either of you – know anything of Louise Chorley?"

"I said I read the papers," said Bernard. "Of course I've heard of her. She shot her husband, didn't she?"

"And you, Miss Gardiner?" said Maitland, ignoring the question.

"I think I've seen her name. I don't read that kind of case, so I don't remember what it was about."

Well, he had asked his questions, and must make what he could of the answers. Now it was time to change the subject. "I believe it's true that in any domestic murder the husband or wife is the first suspect," he said, and saw Geoffrey hide a grin at this ingenuous statement. "But I shouldn't be saying that to you. When is the wedding to be?"

"We've only been engaged a couple of months," said Jacqueline, "and we haven't fixed a day yet. There's a question of finding somewhere to live, somewhere we can

afford. Bernard is an awful stick-in-the-mud about finan-
cial matters, he won't take a chance."

"Money's a serious subject," said Ramsey, half serious,
half amused. He laid his hand over hers suddenly, the first
affectionate gesture that Antony had seen from him.
"We'll see Alan through this first," he said, "then we'll talk
about it seriously."

After that their meal was brought, and while they ate
and for half an hour afterwards they talked of other
things.

Jenny had long since finished her tea when Antony came
upstairs that evening. She saw at once from the stiff way
he moved that he was tired and that his shoulder was
hurting him, and decided regretfully that questions would
have to wait. Also the confession of her own shortcomings
as confidante; which didn't worry her too much, because
he knew well enough after all these years that with anyone
else but Sir Nicholas she'd have given a very good imitation
of a clam.

"You look as if you could do with a drink," she told him.
"Shall I get you one?"

"If you love me," said Antony, and sat down, contrary
to his usual custom, at the opposite end of the sofa to the
one his wife usually occupied.

"You're later than I expected," said Jenny, coming
across the room a moment later with a glass in her hand.

"Am I? After we'd finished with the people at Alan
Kirby's lodgings we looked up Godfrey Thurlow at the
Sefton Gallery, the chap from whom the painting was
stolen in the first place."

"You knew him already, didn't you?"

"Very slightly. Anyway, he was amiable enough but he
couldn't help us. Geoffrey was a little doubtful about the
propriety of going to see him, because I suppose he'll be
identifying the Rubens as his property when Alan Kirby
comes up for trial. But I maintained that as our client isn't
being charged with theft it didn't signify. And whether I'm
right about that or wrong, it doesn't make any difference,
he couldn't help us at all. He'd never heard of Alan Kirby,
or seen him hanging around the gallery. I gather the police

57

had held a sort of identification parade, which may be useful information when we get into court. Not a formal one at the station, they just placed him somewhere where he could watch Alan leave work. But that's really all we learned from him, apart from the fact that he took his loss pretty philosophically while the picture was still missing, being well insured . . . though he says the rates have gone up considerably since there have been so many art thefts in the country. He hasn't got his Rubens back, of course, it's being held as evidence, but he'll be glad enough to see it again in due course."

As he seemed to want to talk, perhaps the ban on questioning might be lifted. "Did you learn anything useful from the other people you saw?" asked Jenny tentatively.

"I learned that Mrs Campbell takes in paying guests, not lodgers. She makes a habit of inspecting visitors, though she doesn't bother when she's sure it's one of her tenants coming home. That if Alan Kirby is telling the truth the most likely date for the canvas to have been planted on him was Sunday, September third, and this is borne out by a senile old man, who has already told a quite different story to the police and who wouldn't be the slightest use in court. I'm not implying he's dishonest, you know, just muddled."

"You mean he saw somebody with the canvas?"

"He says he did."

"But that would help Mr Kirby, wouldn't it?"

"I told you, love, we couldn't use him in court. Ten to one he'd deny the whole thing, in all good faith."

"What does Geoffrey think about it?"

"That it wouldn't help us much anyway, it might have been a delivery made by arrangement. Uncle Nick agrees with him."

"So that's where you've been!"

"Yes, Gibbs was doing his usual hovering act in the hall when I arrived, and gave me the message that Sir Nicholas would like to see me." (Gibbs, that bad tempered anachronism, was an old retainer who flatly refused to be retired, though his duties now were exactly what he chose to do, no more and no less, and he always went to bed sharp at ten.)

"So you know," said Jenny in a hollow voice. Antony steered his left hand along the sofa until it met hers.

"Of course I know, Jenny. If I'd had any sense I wouldn't have asked you to keep quiet about all this."

"Knowing I'm as putty in Uncle Nick's hands," said Jenny more cheerfully.

"That's it exactly. You were right about something else too. He doesn't like things being kept from him, and it would have been much better to be open with him from the beginning. But he and Vera have leaped to the same conclusion that you and Geoffrey did. They're quite sure I'm in a fair way to tangling with this ring of art thieves, which is something I don't agree with any of you about. In fact, I gather from something Vera said that they've been worrying about this so-called organiser ever since March."

"Yes, I thought that too."

"Well, I filled in all the gaps for them, but Uncle Nick isn't pleased, I can tell you that. In fact he spoke his mind very clearly on the subject. I did my best, of course, to convince him that tomorrow will end it until the trial comes on. That seemed to pacify him a little – 'if you mean it', he said – and I left him to Vera's ministrations."

"Yes, thank goodness she's always sympathetic. But do you really mean that, Antony? That after tomorrow –"

"I shall have learned whatever there is to know . . . probably damn all. There's nothing else to be done, love. I've got a nasty feeling that if Alan Kirby goes to prison it will be a great injustice, but I don't see what either Geoffrey or I can do about it."

They left the subject there. Jenny poured him another drink and got one for herself. Roger Farrell came in after dinner, as he so often did after leaving his wife Meg (whose stage name was Margaret Hamilton) at the theatre, and Antony revived sufficiently to enjoy his company. As both he and Jenny generally did, the Farrells were by far their closest friends. But Jenny was uneasy, and aware of a sense of foreboding; she put this down firmly to the fact that she didn't like Antony's being out on Saturday and Sunday, particularly when the long, happy days of the long vacation were still a vivid memory; but later on she was inclined to think she had had a genuine premonition, and it is greatly to her credit that she refrained from saying I told you so.

The Kirbys' house was within easy walking distance of Kempenfeldt Square, in a street Antony knew quite well though he hadn't connected it with them until Geoffrey provided the address. Horton drove into town on Sunday morning, at about a quarter to eleven, and being lucky enough to find a parking space outside number five, left his car in the square. They walked round together to the Kirbys'. "A ruddy mansion," said Antony disagreeably, looking up at it. And indeed it was rather a grand place, and proved to be even more impressive when they were admitted.

In all their time in the house, Antony said later, they didn't see a single piece of furniture that wasn't an antique, or an ornament that wasn't probably almost priceless. But the paintings held pride of place; each one had been carefully hung where it would look its best, and the individual lights focused your attention so that it was quite impossible to avoid the conclusion that to their owner at least they were of very great value.

Mr and Mrs Kirby, they were told by a butler who was almost as old as Gibbs (another relic of the past in all likelihood), were awaiting them in the drawing-room. Antony immediately feared the worst, remembering his two visits to Godfrey Thurlow. The owner of the Sefton Gallery occupied an ugly modern bungalow, but the room in which he received visitors was stiffly furnished with pieces that were probably valuable but even more certainly uncomfortable. However, all was well. There were still the antiques, everything was in its place...no newspapers on the floor, no books lying open on the sofa. But somebody had introduced a number of chairs that were all the most sybaritic could desire. Probably Queen Anne, thought Antony in his ignorance, and never found out whether he was right or not.

Daniel Kirby was a big man, taller and bulkier than his nephew Alan, with rather shaggy hair of an indeterminate

61

sandy shade, and a walrus mustache that had gone one step further and could be described as nothing but ginger. He looked incongruous in the beautiful room, being dressed casually, as if for a day in the country. His wife Hilda, on the other hand, was as neat as a new pin. A tiny, round woman, who reminded Antony vaguely of the redoubtable Mrs Campbell, except that her expression was much gentler.

While Antony was occupied with his observations, Geoffrey, very properly, was making the introductions, and doing his best to explain their presence. For a moment it struck Antony forcibly (his mind was not always well disciplined) that it would be amusing to say directly to their host, We suspect you of being the head of a ring of art thieves, the man Louise Chorley was trying to protect when she shot her husband. But fortunately he had enough self-control to keep this highly slanderous observation to himself. "And as we are very anxious to help Alan," Geoffrey was saying, "his counsel, Mr Maitland, felt he would like to ask you a few questions." Having thus placed the ball squarely in his colleague's court he withdrew metaphorically, leaving Maitland to conduct the interview as best he could.

"Well, of course," said Hilda Kirby. "All we want is to help him. You do understand I hope, both of you, that some terrible mistake has been made."

"If that's so," said Antony, who was sitting near her, "we shall do our best to rectify it. You yourselves are fully convinced of his innocence, then?"

"If the boy has made a fool of himself there's nothing we can do," said Daniel. For the first time it struck Antony what a forceful character Kirby was. He also remembered that Alan thought these two, at least, had faith in him.

"That sounds as if you didn't have quite the same confidence in his integrity that Mrs Kirby does," he said tentatively. Among those present only Geoffrey was aware that the diffident manner was assumed for the occasion.

"The police know their own business, I should have thought. Not that I want to see him go to prison," Kirby added. "Scandal in the family and all that, and after all he's been like a son to us."

62

"More than a son," said Hilda. She had a gentle way of speaking, but there was definitely some rebuke in her tone. "And you know yourself, Daniel, he never had any more interest in art than I have. What would he want with a thing like that?"

"To sell it. Look here, Maitland, what do you know about the background to all this?"

"I'm not sure that I quite understand you."

"Everyone in the art world – my world – knows the number of thefts have been growing over the last few years. Somebody's organising them, that's what it is. And someone might have thought Alan, being my nephew, a worth-while recruit."

"Have you lost anything yourself, Mr Kirby?"

"Not a thing. I take good care of my possessions, don't I? But that might have been the idea."

"Daniel, Daniel, I'm sure you're wrong about that. Alan was grateful to you, you know he was."

"That's as may be. All I know is he had this bee in his bonnet about being a writer, didn't like doing an honest day's job of work."

"But working at it in the evening was so tiring for him," she protested. "Like having two jobs."

"I don't see why. I worked an eighteen-hour day, and sometimes a twenty-hour day when I was his age." Antony remembered that Daniel Kirby had been in his day the proprietor of a very successful chain of grocery stores. Before Alan's grandfather died, that must have been. Presumably, like Mr Jorrocks, he had always had immortal longings in him; for art in his case, not hunting.

"Alan hasn't been charged with theft, Mr Kirby," Antony put in, seeing Hilda silenced for the moment.

"They couldn't prove it, or perhaps he wasn't the actual thief. But the boy's not a fool, you know. He may not have cared for art, as my wife said, but he knew enough to have a pretty good idea what was valuable and what wasn't. Though our opinion is," he added, "that whoever is organising this business knows the market very well indeed."

"Knows who is venal, in fact," said Antony, abandoning caution for the moment. "And who would be quite content to gloat in private over something he knew could never be shown to his friends."

"So you've got that all worked out, have you?"

"It seems obvious."

"I suppose so. There are people like that, you know, I could name a few myself. If I were organising this business I shouldn't need the advice of a young whippersnapper like Alan."

"Daniel, I keep telling you – " Hilda began to remonstrate, and then broke off, shaking her head in a hopeless way.

"He's not worth bothering with," said Daniel firmly. "If we'd had any children of our own you wouldn't make such a fuss over him either."

"Perhaps we might leave the subject of your nephew's possible guilt or innocence," said Antony, the diffident manner very marked again. "I wonder if either of you can tell me of anybody who might have had reason to dislike him."

"If you're thinking the Rubens was planted – " began Daniel aggressively, but this time Hilda interrupted him quite ruthlessly.

"There was that young man where he lives," she said. "Ramsey I think his name is, Bernard Ramsey. He didn't like Alan taking an interest in the girl."

"From what Miss Gardiner told me, that was only the case when he first arrived at Mrs Campbell's. She's engaged to Ramsey now, did you know that?" (God help him, he added to himself.)

"It doesn't surprise me at all. But I must say I'm glad to hear it, she looked a hussy, not good enough for Alan."

"Well, whether that's so or not, she said Alan seemed to lose interest when he saw how things were going between her and Bernard Ramsey. Do you think Ramsey might still have been harbouring some resentment?"

"I wouldn't want to be unjust to anybody," said Hilda Kirby doubtfully, "but you did ask us about that, and he's the only person I can think of."

"What about you, Mr Kirby?"

"I can see you're worried by the same point that's worrying the rest of us... those of us with any sense that is," he added, with a look at his wife that could only be regarded as venomous. "If Alan's telling the truth, if he didn't know the painting was in his room, somebody must have planted it there deliberately to implicate him. He's a very unimportant young man, I can't see that either his work at Holiday Press, or his aspirations as a writer, could involve him in a predicament like that."

Maitland was beginning to have considerable respect for Daniel Kirby's intellect, but he neither confirmed nor denied his supposition. "I was hoping you might have some ideas that would help us," he said. And then, changing the subject with some abruptness, and making no attempt to lead into the new one tactfully, "Alan says you know Louise Chorley."

Hilda started to say something but Daniel overrode her ruthlessly. "So you had heard about the art thefts before I mentioned them, and David Chorley's connection with them into the bargain," he said. "I read the account of the inquest on him, which I suppose is where you got your information, and of course the art world – which is a silly label, though I keep using it – has talked of nothing else but this organisation ever since."

"Yes, I read the account of the inquest," said Maitland, truthfully enough. "But you didn't answer my question."

"Well, of course we knew her. She was a very good friend of Hilda's. And why I'm talking about the poor woman as if she were dead I can't imagine."

"I suppose because she might as well be," said Hilda gloomily. "It's such a shock when something like that happens to people you know. First there was hearing that David had been shot, and then that Louise had been arrested, and after that that he was a murderer himself. I suppose the shock of hearing about it just turned her mind."

"Yes, I think that's the most charitable view to take," said Daniel Kirby, who hadn't been showing any great signs of that particular virtue up to then. "Anyway we've been approached by her lawyer to act as character witnesses."

"It's none of my business, but have you agreed?"

"Naturally. As Hilda says the poor woman must have

65

been deranged by shock. She was a very gentle person you know, all those poems... absolute drivel, but at least they show how her mind works."

"I suppose you're right. Well, I think that's all we can do here, Geoffrey."

"Yes," said Geoffrey, rising, "we're grateful for your time."

"Do your best for the boy," said Daniel unexpectedly. "You know I'll cover all the charges."

Hilda followed them out into the hall. "Don't take any notice of Daniel when he's being horrid," she told them, "he's really very fond of Alan. Well, you heard what he said about paying for his defence, he means it you know, but if he didn't I would, of course."

"Thank you, Mrs Kirby, we shall do our best for him, you can be sure of that." Maitland's farewells were rather perfunctory, and it was left to Horton to express their gratitude in due form. "What's biting you?" he asked, as soon as they were out on the pavement again.

"What makes you think—?"

"I haven't known you all these years for nothing," said Geoffrey bluntly. "You've had an idea, and I'd like to know what it is."

"In case it involves you?" Maitland's inflection was humorous. "It's too vague to put into words really. I was just thinking that Kevin O'Brien can't possibly call the Walpoles, or any of their set who knew Louise Chorley, for evidence about her character."

"Well, of course he can't!" said Geoffrey impatiently. "I don't know what that has to do with anything."

"Neither do I, I suppose. Forget it, Geoffrey." He glanced at his watch and lengthened his stride a little. "Jenny's expecting us for lunch, do you remember? After which I suppose we'll have two equally wasted interviews with the Shields and the Connollys."

Their appointment with Raymond Shields and his wife, Constance, was not until two-thirty, so they were able to take their time over the meal. This time Geoffrey took his car; the Shields lived in Chelsea, not far from the Farrells' house. Not a grand place like the Kirby mansion, but definitely a good address.

It was Constance Shields who let them in, a tall, redheaded woman; no beauty, but with a lot of character in her face. She took them into a long, narrow room, with no pretensions to anything but comfort, and introduced them to her husband, Raymond. He was shorter than his wife by a good four inches, with a round benevolent face. Antony had the thought, not altogether charitable, that he could imagine Raymond and Louise Chorley getting on like a house on fire over the matter of the latter's poetry.

He greeted them jovially enough. "Well, well, it's a great pleasure, though I can't imagine how we can help you," he said. He looked from one of them to the other. "I'm afraid I haven't quite sorted out yet which of you is which."

"I'm Alan Kirby's solicitor," said Geoffrey, and repeated his name. "And this is his counsel, Antony Maitland." To Antony's relief no sign of recognition dawned in the other man's eyes.

"Well, I have to say it's interesting. That's what I told you, isn't it, my dear?" he added to his wife. "But I can't think," he said again, "what you can expect us to do for you. We don't know very much about Alan really."

"He's a sort of connection," said Constance. "That is, I'm Hilda Kirby's cousin. And, of course, I know her very well, and Dan."

"Have you known them for long?"

"I said I was Hilda's cousin, didn't I? I've known her all my life, and Daniel ever since they were married."

"Then you must have known Alan when he lived with them for a while."

"Certainly I did. And so did Ray, though not so well. But we never believed anything like this could possibly happen."

"You see," said Geoffrey, "there's the question of character references. He's never been in any trouble before, and that might be very important. Would you be willing to appear for the defence in that connection?" He looked from one of them to the other as he spoke, dividing the question between them.

"That's funny," said Raymond. "It's only the other day a similar request was made to us."

"What sort of a request?" asked Antony quickly.

"To give character evidence on behalf of someone we know very well. Louise Chorley, to be exact."

"Did you agree?"

"Yes, of course we did. And I think Connie may have misled you, when she said she knew Alan better than I did. On a personal basis, of course, that's true, she's known him longer than I have. But, after all, he worked for me."

"So perhaps—"

"It's a little difficult. Up to the time of his arrest I could have given you a positive answer, he'd never do anything dishonest. But then you get thinking, you know, he didn't really like the work he was doing, wanted to write himself and go in for a good deal deeper research than is permissible in our line. So he might have been desperate for money."

"Oh, no, I don't think that at all," said Constance. "It's a thing all young people have to face up to, going slowly at first, working their way towards the things they're ambitious about. I'm quite certain Alan would have been content to do that."

"So you would be willing, Mrs Shields, to give evidence as to his good character? And you, perhaps," he added, turning to Raymond, "about his work?"

"I'd go on record as vouching for his conscientiousness," said Shields firmly. "When I said he didn't really care for the job he was doing, I didn't mean he didn't give a day's work for a day's pay. Will that help?"

"I think that's something we have to give some thought to," said Antony, looking enquiringly at Geoffrey, who nodded. "You had his address at the office, I suppose. Have either of you visited him there?"

"I'd been to tea one weekend," Constance replied. "With Hilda, you know. It wasn't grand," she added firmly, "but I think he'd made himself quite comfortable, and I'm sure he preferred being independent."

So she was clever enough to see where questions on that score might lead. "And you, Mr Shields?" Antony enquired.

"I'd only been there once, and that was the Saturday before all this blew up. There was a book that had to get to the printers if we were going to do it at all, but Alan had a feeling he'd seen something on the same subject before, and wanted to root about among his possessions at home to see if he was right. I phoned on the Saturday morning, as I said, and then went round to talk the matter over. He recommended publishing, even though he had found this previous book. Our author had come across a few new facts, and an attractive way of presenting them."

"I believe Alan Kirby is mainly concerned with historical matters . . . anything remotely connected with history, I suppose you'd say. But that isn't the only kind of book you publish?"

"No, we go in for cookbooks and books on gardening, and we do a very comprehensive line of greeting cards. And of course, there used to be Louise Chorley's poems. They were a very popular item."

"Popular and profitable," said Constance.

"Didn't you like them, Mrs Shields?"

"Well, you must admit, they're sentiment of the worst kind," said Constance. "But there, that was Louise all over, or I thought it was until all this happened."

"My wife is something of a highbrow," said Raymond apologetically. "That's why she gets on with Dan Kirby like a house on fire, she knows his subject backwards."

"I'm the merest amateur," Constance protested.

"Well, I know you didn't get paid for the work" – from Shields's tone this might have been a source of grievance – "but Kirby thought enough of your knowledge to get you to catalogue his collection, which was no easy task, and obviously you did all right because I know you've been keeping it up to date ever since."

"Well, yes," she agreed. "All the same–"

"All the same, you agreed, I believe you said, to give character evidence on Mrs Chorley's behalf."

"Well, of course, I'll do what I can for the poor thing."

"But not quite so willingly as you'd speak for Alan Kirby?"

"I suppose that's right. You're putting words into my

mouth, Mr Maitland, but I think I have to agree with you."

They talked for some time after that, and Constance offered tea which the visitors refused. "I can't say," said Maitland as they made their way back to the car, "that our efforts today have done much to enhance our client's prospects."

"I'm afraid you're right," said Geoffrey, "but did you really think they would?"

"No," said Antony, and sighed. "And don't for the love of heaven, Geoffrey, say At least we're doing our best."

"All right, I won't," said Horton, unlocking the car. "You'll find the map book in the glove compartment, Antony. The Connollys live somewhere out in the sticks."

For a change it was a modern house, on a so-far-unfinished estate in North London. Somebody had done a good job of denuding the terrain of trees, and it would be a good many years before the place looked presentable again. As to price, Antony judged they would be in the medium range. The Connollys' garden had not yet been made, in fact it looked as if they would have considerable trouble in getting rid of some patches of concrete left by the builders. There were also a number of piles of rather clayey soil, more easily dealt with probably, but still depressing.

Connolly let them in. Rather a nondescript man really, probably almost as tall as Daniel Kirby but much more slightly built. He shared with Raymond Shields, however, a welcoming look, seeming genuinely pleased to see them. Geoffrey was apologising because they were a little later than he had said, but Ernest Connolly waved this aside.

"Nothing better to do," he said, and then grinned at his own ineptitude. "Things that might have been put differently," he remarked. "Come in and meet the wife."

Maria Connolly was without doubt a dowdy woman, and also, as they soon discovered, one of the martyrs of this world. "So lucky it was this afternoon you wanted to see us," she said earnestly, getting up to shake hands. "All the children are out, I wouldn't want them to be mixed up in anything nasty."

70

Antony and Geoffrey took this implied slur on their powers of discretion calmly. "How many children have you?" asked Antony, feeling that this much interest was expected of him.

"Four, three boys and a girl. That's why we moved, you need more room as they get bigger, as I expect you both know. Now I'm going to make you some tea, I won't take No for an answer, and Ernest can say just what he likes to you while I'm gone."

Connolly seemed in no hurry to avail himself of this invitation. "I gather your visit concerns Alan Kirby," he said, rather hesitantly now. "Quite frankly I agreed to our meeting because I was interested to see you both, but I don't understand how I can help you."

"It's a matter of character evidence," said Geoffrey, ignoring Maitland's scowl. "You must understand that it might make quite a difference in this particular case."

"But I scarcely knew him, and my wife had never met him at all."

"I'm sorry. I didn't realise your acquaintance was so slight," said Geoffrey. "I believe you'd visited him at his lodgings."

"Yes, I did, I forget the exact date. He had written to the paper with a suggestion for a series of articles, and I was interested in them. However, it was rather difficult to see him during the day because of his job, so I promised to call on him one evening."

"Were you able to reach an agreement?" Maitland took over the questioning.

"Yes, in fact if either of you take *The Courier*, you'll have seen two or three of the articles already. Whether they'll ever be finished, of course, is another matter."

"Perhaps somebody else—"

"Yes, perhaps."

"You must have spent a little time with Alan Kirby making sure he was a suitable person to write for you. What did you gather about his interests?"

"I think I should say they were rather narrow. I had hoped – Daniel Kirby's nephew you know – that he might have acquired a liking, or at least some knowledge of painting from his uncle."

71

"Is that one of your interests, then?" But it should have been obvious. There was a coffee-table sized book on the sofa, on whose cover the word "Corot" was the only one large enough to be read.

"An interest, yes, and that's where it has to stay." He smiled suddenly. "You carefully avoided looking around the room when you said that, Mr Maitland. When I want to indulge in my hobby I have to go to an art gallery."

"Is there any particular period you favour?" said Antony, assuming an interest he did not feel.

"I think I may say I have a catholic taste, but no money to indulge it. Perhaps that's just as well, Maria doesn't share my views on the subject."

Mrs Connolly came back into the room at that moment, and caught the end of the remark. "I should say not," she said, putting down the tray. "Dust traps, that's all pictures are. As if there wasn't enough work about the house already."

"I'm sure with four children–"

"Yes, you understand." Maitland assumed an almost impossible look of virtue. "Nothing but work all day, while Ernest here goes off to his office like a lord."

"Yes, Mr Connolly," – Geoffrey was anxious to get the conversation back on its pre-ordained rails before his companion lost sight of the point of their meeting altogether – "you said you thought Alan Kirby's interests were strictly limited."

"To historical matters, I mean. But there you are, like me he can't afford to do just as he likes. Research, that would be his field I imagine. He can't really enjoy working for the Holiday Press."

"Are you implying... thank you, Mrs Connolly, a cup of tea is just what we need, isn't it, Geoffrey? Are you implying that your job is equally distasteful to you?"

"I think that's too strong a word. There are advantages, a wide circle of acquaintances for instance."

"You never bring them home," said Maria.

"I didn't think you were interested, my dear." Connolly's tone was suddenly silky. "Besides it would just be more work for you."

"Have you any acquaintance with Louise Chorley?" said

72

Maitland, sipping his tea. It was just as he disliked it most, very strong and milky, and he thought he'd better get the most important question before the meeting before it made him quite literally sick.

It was Maria Connolly who got in with her reply first. "Louise Chorley," she said, clasping her hands together. "Now there's a woman I admire tremendously. I was so pleased when her solicitor asked us to give evidence on her behalf."

"To be character witnesses? Did you agree?"

"Yes, of course. I admit, I had to persuade Ernest. But it's quite impossible that she should have done what they say she did, such a beautiful soul!"

"Now how...oh, yes, of course, you were connected with the Selden prosecution, weren't you?" asked Connolly. "I know Louise too, though I'm afraid my admiration for her isn't quite as unbridled as my wife's. *The Courier* publishes her poems, you know, or did when there were any to publish."

"Was it your job to pass judgement on them?"

"Not precisely. If you want a description of my work...oh, well, you won't want technicalities. Let's just say I'm responsible for the layout of the editorial page and the one opposite. When I had a gap to fill, which happens more often than you would think, there was a good chance that one of Louise's poems would do the trick."

"That's a dreadful way to think of them," said Mrs Connolly, quite horrified. "She's a wonderful woman and—"

"And a self-confessed murderess," said Connolly, rather brutally.

"You mentioned Daniel Kirby a few moments ago," said Antony hastily. "Do you know him?"

"By reputation, very well. And I have been introduced to him, though I doubt if he'd remember."

"And Raymond Shields?"

"The same answer would stand. I've met him, of course, but you could hardly call it a friendship. He has a very knowledgeable wife, knowledgeable about my hobby I mean. I think if I knew her better I should find her more sympathetic."

That brought another outburst from Maria, under cover of which the two visitors got to their feet. "I'm sorry we've wasted your time, Mr Connolly," said Geoffrey, and hoped that his hostess wouldn't notice Antony's almost untouched cup of tea, so that they could get away without any further outcry.

Geoffrey elected to go straight home, instead of stopping for tea in Kempenfeldt Square, but he dropped Antony off outside number five on his way. Maitland found, as he had expected, his uncle and Vera taking tea with Jenny, and as Sir Nicholas had already finished off the buttered toast he judged that they had nearly finished. Jenny jumped up and offered to make a fresh pot, but he declined with a shudder, the memory of Mrs Connolly's brew being still over-vivid in his mind. "Where are Roger and Meg?" he asked. The Farrells were usually with them at this time on a Sunday, and often stayed on to dinner, as it was Meg's one free evening.

"Don't you remember, Antony? They were making a flying visit to Grunning's Hole, to close the cottage up for the winter, I suppose. They're just staying overnight."

"Yes, I remember now. Roger's come to the conclusion that what he calls 'that damn play' is going to run for ever," he confided to Vera. "And as it isn't really teatime any more, may I get anyone a drink?"

"You're evading the issue, Antony," said Sir Nicholas lazily, from the depths of his favourite chair, the wing chair on the right of the fireplace. "Here we are, all agog to hear your adventures, and all we get instead is an account of Jenny's dreams."

"What dreams?" Antony demanded of his wife.

"Only one," said Jenny. "I only mentioned it because it was rather comical. I dreamed I was talking to a penguin, and saying to it, You'd be much better eating fish rather than trying to make a pudding. Do you suppose it had some tremendous significance?"

"Something too awful to contemplate, I should imagine," said Antony, smiling at her. "As for adventures, Uncle Nick, there weren't any, and in their absence I doubt if you'd be interested in our doings."

74

"As long as you had Geoffrey with you I'm not too worried," said his uncle. "Interest is another matter."

"Well, we talked to all three people, outside Mrs Campbell's household, whom Alan Kirby remembered having visited him and who therefore knew the way to his room."

"Four," said Jenny, "You're forgetting Mrs Kirby, his aunt."

"No, I'm not. If I must be accurate, her cousin, Mrs Shields, went with her on one occasion. But for one reason and another I'm more interested in the men."

"Mrs Chorley's lover," said Sir Nicholas nodding his head. "You're not overlooking the fact, I suppose, that Alan Kirby may have forgotten all about somebody, even some quite frequent visitor."

"No, I realise that, Uncle Nick. The thing is I've got to start somewhere. Or rather I thought I had."

"What do you mean by that?" asked Vera in her gruff way.

"Just that there wasn't an interesting fact to be had out of the lot of them."

"I'd be interested to know," said Sir Nicholas, "what excuse you made for calling on these gentlemen."

"Well, it was quite natural to call on the Kirbys, they're my client's uncle and aunt. As to the others, Geoffrey was rather clever about that, I thought. He said there was a question of calling them as character witnesses. And that might not have been a bad idea in the case of Raymond Shields, except for the fact that he seems to be extremely doubtful about Alan's innocence. His wife is another matter, she's quite certain he wouldn't do a thing like that." He brought out the phrase with rather savage mockery. "But Ernest Connolly was the merest acquaintance of his."

"All the same, you may as well tell us," Sir Nicholas suggested.

"All right, here goes." Even with his uncle's interruptions – Sir Nicholas seemed to be in a captious mood that day – the story wasn't a long one. "So you see," Maitland concluded, "we're no further forward at all and there isn't another thing to be done until we get into court. And when we do . . . well the Rubens was certainly stolen goods, and it was certainly found in Alan Kirby's wardrobe."

"Then I suggest," said Sir Nicholas, "that we clear all this away" – waving a hand to encompass the tea things – "and have that drink you mentioned." He watched benevolently while Vera and Jenny tidied up and his nephew poured sherry, but made no attempt at all to take part in the proceedings. "We're staying to dinner, Antony," he went on, as Maitland placed a glass at his elbow. "Jenny'd forgotten too about Meg and Roger being away, so we agreed to help out. Pure altruism, so that you don't have to eat leftovers tomorrow."

"That was kind of you," said Antony dryly.

"Also," said Vera coming back into the room, and sitting down heavily in the corner of the sofa nearest her husband's chair, "there happened to be a film Mrs Stokes particularly wanted to see, so she's out this evening."

"That explains it." As indeed it did. For many years Sir Nicholas had been taking refuge with the Maitlands whenever his housekeeper took the evening off. He had told Jenny once that he never could understand how a woman who cooked like an angel on most occasions went completely to pieces when faced with the prospect of preparing a cold collation. "Anyway, you're very welcome to share our board," said Antony magnanimously, "so long as you don't want to talk shop."

"There doesn't seem to be much point in it, does there?" said his uncle gently. And continued, dividing the reassurance between Jenny and Vera, "I don't think his activities so far can have done much harm."

So the evening was a peaceful one, and gradually Antony's self-irritation with his lack of success was soothed. Vera said it was an evening for Mozart, and made a personal selection from the Maitlands' records. One way and another it was later than usual when she and Sir Nicholas got up to go. The little gold clock on the mantelpiece had just struck eleven in its rather tinkling way.

But before they were half way to the door the phone rang. Jenny said, "I'll get it," and Antony followed his uncle and aunt out into the hall. But they hadn't reached

76

the front door when Jenny's voice followed them in agitation, "Antony, come quickly!" and they all turned back into the living-room again.

Maitland, as might have been expected, reached his wife's side more quickly than the others. "What's the matter, love?" he asked urgently.

"It's Geoffrey," said Jenny. "I think you'd better talk to him."

"Your teeth are chattering," said Antony accusingly. "I thought that was just a figure of speech, I didn't think it ever happened."

"Just talk to Geoffrey," she pleaded.

"All right." He took the receiver from her hand. "What's the matter now?" he enquired, not too patiently.

"I'm talking from the morgue on Lennox Street." Even Horton's calm had been somewhat shaken. "The police called me in to identify Alan Kirby, as none of his friends from the boarding-house were at home and he had my address in his notebook."

"Identify him?" said Antony sharply.

"Yes, he's dead. He was shot in the street from a passing car, about three hours ago."

There was no question then of the visitors leaving, they settled themselves round the fire again – it was colder that evening – and Antony made another round with the cognac, even pouring some for Jenny against her protests because he felt she needed it. Though he was well enough aware that what was upsetting her was the fact that he would no longer consider his obligations to his client over, rather than Alan Kirby's death.

"There are several things I want to know," said Sir Nicholas, cradling his glass in his hands. "To begin with, where was he shot?"

"In Bramley Street, I gather, no more than a few hundred yards from Mrs Campbell's front door. But if you mean, Uncle Nick, did the car draw up and the driver shoot him, and then drive away, or was it more like a gangland killing, with one man driving and one man spraying the street with bullets, Geoffrey didn't tell me. I don't suppose he knew."

"Like to have your opinion," said Vera. "Does this make his guilt more or less likely?"

"Oh Lord, I don't know." Maitland sounded suddenly weary. "I don't think there's a ha'p'orth to choose either way, if you consider his death in a vacuum, as it were. But taking everything into account I still think he was most likely innocent; his guilt raises too many questions."

"At least," said his uncle with quiet satisfaction, "there's nothing more you can do in the matter."

"Uncle Nick!" Antony turned on him angrily. "Don't you see that's the one thing I can't do, give up now? It's because of my damnable interference that he's been killed."

"Let's examine the logic of that for a moment."

"It's perfectly logical. I've been asking questions all the weekend, and so has Geoffrey. Someone's afraid of what we'll find out. And if you think I can wrap the whole thing up and forget that Alan Kirby ever existed, you've got another think coming."

For once in his life Sir Nicholas took no notice of the colloquialism. "My dear boy, you must be reasonable," he said.

"I don't feel reasonable," said Antony.

"No, I can see that. You've lost your temper," said his uncle coldly.

"What the hell do you expect?"

"I expect you to exercise some restraint," said Sir Nicholas, at his most austere. Jenny and Vera exchanged an uneasy glance. "What you must realise, however, is that you've no shadow of an excuse for asking any more questions."

"If only I were in Kevin O'Brien's shoes—"

"You insist on connecting this latest happening too with Louise Chorley's lover?"

"Uncle Nick, I think there must be a connection. Oh, I know there was Bernard Ramsey too who could have planted the painting on Alan, but I can't really see him as the spider at the centre of the web."

"There's nothing to say that the spider, as you call him, acted himself either in the matter of planting the painting on young Kirby or in the matter of killing him."

"I've got to start somewhere," said Antony despairingly, as he had done before.

"I see no reason for you to start at all."

There was a short silence after that. "Who's handling the prosecution?" asked Antony suddenly.

"If you mean when Mrs Chorley comes to trial, I understand it will be Halloran."

"Yes, I'd a feeling it might be his sort of case." (Bruce Halloran was a close friend of Sir Nicholas's, a man whose finger was never very far from the pulse of the legal community.) "A man not amenable to suggestion," Antony added sadly. And then, on a more hopeful note, "Oh well, I expect I shall think of something."

"And the trouble is, I expect he will," said Sir Nicholas to his wife, a little later when they were downstairs again in their own quarters. "If I could only persuade him to leave well alone... and to try and act on such flimsy evidence too."

"You must admit he's been right in these matters more often than he's been wrong."

"But he has been wrong," said Sir Nicholas stubbornly.

"What sort of an effect does that have on him?" asked Vera, shrewdly putting her finger on what her husband realised now was the whole point of the discussion.

"I don't know if you realise it, my dear, though I think you probably do, but Antony is not always inclined to trust his own judgement."

"You'd never think it to look at him," said Vera. "Oh, I've noticed that diffident air he puts on when dealing with a witness – he's done it once or twice in cases we've been working on together – but I always supposed it was completely unreal. Isn't it?"

"You're quite right about that, of course. As far as his profession is concerned he's quite capable of a bit of play-acting. But he jumps to conclusions about his client's guilt or innocence... and you must admit it's often pure guesswork, Vera. That wouldn't be so bad if it meant he was absolutely certain he was right; the trouble is he dithers between the two points of view. Which is painful for the onlooker, because it is so intensely painful to him."

79

"Know what you mean," said Vera. "Watched it myself on several occasions. You also mean, I suppose," she went on gruffly, "that if he's wrong it just makes it worse for him next time."

"I mean exactly that."

"All the same, nothing for it but to give him his head. If you don't want Alan Kirby's ghost to haunt him for the rest of his life," she added, with a sudden, unexpected flight of imagination.

"And how, my dear, do you propose I should do that?"

"You might start by telling him about Bruce Halloran's colleague," said Vera, for once in her life not looking directly at her husband.

"About – ? Do you know what you're saying, Vera?"

"Only that Antony has some idea in his head about these people who've been called as character witnesses on Louise Chorley's behalf," said Vera.

"So you think that's what Antony meant by those highly cryptic remarks of his?" said Sir Nicholas thoughtfully.

"I'm sure of it."

"And you're in favour of giving him his head, to repeat your own words on the subject." Sir Nicholas smiled at her suddenly. "I seem to remember, my dear, there were occasions in the past when Antony's methods made you nervous."

"While I was working with him myself," Vera admitted. "But that was different."

"The trouble is," her husband sighed, "I find myself unable to take quite so objective a view of his activities."

"Think you must try," said Vera seriously.

"By telling him that the counsel who was going to assist Halloran in the prosecution has got a ruptured appendix?" said Sir Nicholas.

"Said that, didn't I? But of course it wouldn't do. What you ought to do is talk to Halloran himself about it. He might be only too glad –"

"I'm not quite sure it would be altogether proper for Antony to concern himself in this particular prosecution."

"If you're meaning that he was connected with the

Selden case," said Vera, who saw no reason to pretend to misunderstand him, "nobody knows about that. Besides, this is nothing to do with David Chorley's crimes, except as they provided a motive, only with something that happened after Antony had relinquished all interest in the matter."

"I suppose you're right," said Sir Nicholas and sighed again. "Though I still can't agree it was wise for him to drag Geoffrey to see the owner of the Sefton Gallery."

"Injudicious," Vera agreed. "But it doesn't matter now that Alan Kirby's dead."

"Just one more example of how wrong-headed he can be," Sir Nicholas grumbled. "But you remember our previous talk, Vera. If one of these men is the organiser, it could be dangerous to go any further with the investigation."

"Trouble is," said Vera, who didn't believe in being over-subtle, "he's not going to be happy unless he does. You don't want him blaming himself for the rest of his life for Alan Kirby's murder, do you?"

"Anything but that."

"Well, I dare say he will," said Vera, not very consolingly. "But it might be a comfort to him to ... well, to revenge his death."

"You're being melodramatic, Vera."

"But realistic," she insisted.

"Very well then, my dear, I'll do what I can." Once persuaded, Sir Nicholas wasted no time in indecision. "I'll talk to Halloran first thing in the morning," he promised.

Monday, 2nd October

Meanwhile Antony, in the early hours of the morning, had formed a plan as to how he himself should proceed. This involved a telephone call to Scotland Yard as soon as he got to chambers, and he was lucky in finding Detective Chief Inspector Sykes at his desk. "Any chance of having a word with you this morning?" he enquired without preamble.

Sykes, however, was not to be put off his careful enquiries about Jenny's health and Sir Nicholas's and Vera's. He was a great man for the proprieties. At any other time Maitland would have been amused; this morning he just found this politeness irritating, and answered as briefly as he could. "I *do* want to see you, Chief Inspector," he said, as soon as he thought the detective was in the mood to listen.

"Yes, Mr Maitland, so you said. I take it it's about your late client, Alan Kirby."

"Yes, it is."

"I wonder what exactly your interest is. You've no further standing in the matter that I know of."

"Neither had Geoffrey Horton, but you called him last night."

"Yes, we were in something of a dilemma. Neither Mrs Campbell nor her niece seemed an appropriate person to call on for an identification, and the only other man in the place – except for old Mr Brewster, of course – was nowhere to be found. You've met them all, I gather, so you'll realise our predicament."

"Yes, I do. But what about his uncle?"

"Daniel Kirby was out somewhere."

"I see. Are you yourself handling Alan's murder?"

"It so happens that I am, but –"

"Don't tell me again I've no standing in the matter. I'm quite aware of it. I think you might allow me a little ordinary human curiosity though."

"Is that all it is?" Sykes sounded sceptical. But then he

relented; afterwards Maitland was to become certain that it was for some purpose of his own. "Well, I've no objection to talking to you, Mr Maitland. Would you like to come here to see me?"

"You know I hate the place. If you don't want the bother of coming all the way here, we could have a cup of coffee on some neutral ground."

Sykes agreed, and suggested, after no more than a moment's hesitation – as Antony had known he would – a meeting place that he thought would be suitable. "Ten minutes' walk for you," he said, "and about the same time in a taxi for me. Will that do you, Mr Maitland?"

"Excellently well, and I'm very much obliged to you."

"As to that," said Sykes, preparing to ring off, "you'd better save your gratitude until we've had our talk. You may feel differently after that."

Antony arrived at the café first, selected a corner table, and ordered coffee while he waited for his companion to join him. It was still early, and the place was almost empty; not much to distract his attention, but Sykes arrived almost immediately. The detective was a square-built man, who looked far more like a farmer than a police officer. A prosperous farmer, who had done a good deal at that day's market perhaps. That was the simile that always came into Antony's head, and the slow North Country accent did nothing to dispel the illusion. For all that he had a great respect for Sykes's intellect, and something akin to friendship had grown between them throughout the years. Each had had occasion from time to time to feel a sense of obligation towards the other; and as both were conscientious men, each was inclined to regard his own obligation as the more serious.

Even now there was no hurrying Skyes. He settled himself comfortably in his chair, ordered coffee and chocolate biscuits, and gave his companion his sedate smile. "It must be quite six months since we met, Mr Maitland," he observed. "How do you find yourself?"

"You asked me that already," said Maitland.

"No, I don't think so. I enquired after Mrs Maitland's health, and wondered how your uncle and aunt were getting on, but we didn't discuss you."

"Well, there's no need. I'm perfectly well." Then he grinned suddenly. "But curious," he added.

"I can't say that surprises me, knowing you," said Sykes. "And I'm not saying there aren't a few things I want to say to you, even apart from answering your questions. So what I'd like to suggest is a *quid pro quo*. You answer my questions, and I'll answer yours as far as I can."

"If you mean, that I shall agree to answer your questions whatever they may be, while you pick and choose among mine, there's nothing doing!"

"Don't be so legal-minded," Sykes admonished him. "You'll exercise your judgement as you see it, I know that well enough. But I also know that there's nothing in my questions that you can't properly answer. Until I hear what they are, I can't say the same about yours."

"Very well." There was a pause while the second cup of coffee was brought. "Do you always eat these things at this time of the morning?" asked Antony, reaching for a chocolate biscuit. "You'll be putting on weight if you do."

"I thought they might do you good," said Sykes demurely, helping himself in his turn. "Did that 'very well' mean that you agree to my proposition?"

"Oh yes, I'm curious about that too now."

"You asked me if I was investigating Alan Kirby's death. I am, but I understand he was awaiting trial, and that you were to be his counsel."

"That's perfectly correct. And don't tell me you haven't your own methods, Chief Inspector, of finding out what the case against him was and all the details of the prosecution, because I wouldn't believe you."

"No, of course I've heard the official version. What does interest me though is the fact that you were making some enquiries about what seems to have been a very straightforward case. Not only that, you persuaded Mr Horton to go along with you."

"I see. If I told you Geoffrey doesn't think I'm safe to be out alone you wouldn't believe me, I suppose."

"I might at that," said Sykes seriously. "However, I think his presence indicates that you had some doubts about your client's guilt."

84

"Very serious doubts."

"How did they arise?"

"I don't know that I'm at liberty to tell you that. No, I'm not trying to hold out on you, Chief Inspector, I'll do my best to explain. Something was said that brought to my mind the possibility – this was a case where an art theft was involved, remember – that the charge against Alan Kirby might in some way be involved with what happened last March, and what Louise Chorley did to protect the man she said was her lover."

"What has Sir Nicholas to say about that?" asked Sykes, smiling.

"Jumping to conclusions as usual." His mimicry of his uncle was wickedly exact. "But he's used to me, you know. I do see one very great objection to the theory that Alan Kirby was innocent: why should anyone want to frame him? On the other hand, if he was guilty why did someone give him away to the police?"

"I'm sure you have an answer to that one, Mr Maitland."

"When thieves fall out," said Antony promptly, with at that moment only a vague feeling that he had heard the phrase used before not very long ago. "All the same I'll tell you one thing, Geoffrey and I got a very different story from Mr Brewster from the one he gave to the police. That's not to say he was lying on either occasion, he's practically senile. We couldn't have used his evidence, but he said he saw somebody enter the house with a canvas under his arm. He added that it was a weekend, because Alan Kirby wasn't at work and had just gone out about five minutes before. Also that it was drizzling. That would put it on Sunday, September the third, and the fact that I could confirm so much with young Kirby made me think that perhaps the old man was right."

"Even if he was, the painting might have been delivered by arrangement."

"Yes, so one person after another has been telling me," said Antony impatiently. "So I'll tell you something else. Making the assumption, which I'm the first to admit may be unjustified, that he was being framed, I asked Alan Kirby who, apart from the household at Mrs Campbell's, knew where his room was. He'd had very few visitors; in fact, apart from his aunt Hilda who used to go to tea with him at weekends quite often, he could think of only three. All three have been asked to give character evidence in Louise Chorley's defence."

That silenced Sykes for a moment. "Now you do interest me, Mr Maitland," he said. "Who were these three men, I wonder."

"Daniel Kirby, Alan's uncle. Raymond Shields, who owns the Holiday Press, where Alan worked. And Ernest Connolly, an editor on *The Courier*, for whom Alan was doing a series of historical articles."

"Do all these people know each other?"

"The Kirbys and the Shields quite well, I believe; Mrs Kirby and Mrs Shields are cousins. Mrs Connolly, I must admit, is a sort of odd man out, I don't think she knew any of the others. Her husband knew them by reputation, and had met both Shields and Kirby, but that was as far as it went."

"And that was the extent of your researches?"

"Oh, I talked to everybody who lived in the house, and I did hear some story that Bernard Ramsey and Alan Kirby had been after the same girl at one time, so there might be some resentment there. But as Ramsey and the girl concerned are now engaged, it seems unlikely that he should really be harbouring any resentment. Besides, I quite frankly can't take him seriously as the organiser of those art thefts you told me about six months ago."

"So that's what's in your mind," said Sykes, as though this confirmed his worst fears. "But I told you then and I tell you again now, Mr Maitland, that isn't a safe game to play. Particularly now, when you have no client to worry about."

"Is that how you see it?" Antony's tone was suddenly cutting. "The way I look at it, Sykes, is that Alan Kirby was killed because I was asking questions. If that doesn't make me responsible I don't know what does."

"That's nonsense and you know it," said Sykes at his most blunt.

"Is that why you wanted to see me? To warn me?"

"That was one of the reasons. If what happened to Alan Kirby isn't enough for you –"

"It was the first time any killing has been involved with these art thefts, wasn't it?"

"You're still going too fast for me, Mr Maitland, unless" – Sykes's eyes were suddenly suspicious – "you know something that you're keeping to yourself."

"I'm working purely on guesswork, Chief Inspector. In my uncle's absence I can admit that to you. But it does seem likely that there's some connection, don't you think?"

"Well, allowing for the moment that there is, this isn't the first occasion on which violence has been done."

"Six months ago you informed me –"

"This happened since then. You know how I told you we thought the thing was worked: one man organising the whole, a man, of course, of considerable knowledge, with a small band of helpers to carry out the actual thefts. David Chorley was one of these latter, and actually had a painting in his house for a few days at one time. I think that must have been the difficult part, disposing of the goods when they were received. Though I'm also convinced that nothing was stolen until there was a market for it."

"A man with collecting fever badly enough to pay good money for something he could never show to anybody else," Antony agreed. "Still, I can see the difficulty in transporting these things until the hue and cry had died down."

"Well, that happened to an old lag called Clark, known predictably enough as Nobby. It's really rather a funny story, Mr Maitland, though it has a tragic ending. He became an informer and was knocked off by the gang. That was their first killing."

"What did he tell you?" asked Antony eagerly.

"Not the identity of the man on top, if that's what you're wondering. His contact was David Chorley, and Chorley's death left him with a picture on his hands and nobody to pass it on to. It was an intensely modernistic painting, a woman with three eyes, or something like that, and though he shut it away in a cupboard those eyes were

87

following him all over his room. Finally he could bear it no longer, and came to us. Though I must admit he also had in mind the fact that a pretty good reward had been offered for the return of the painting."

"So they killed him."

"Yes, it was a pity, he wasn't a bad little chap. I came into it after the killing, of course, and I must admit to you, Mr Maitland – though I'm afraid this will only help to convince you – that the killing was done in much the same way as what happened last night."

"It does tend to convince me," said Antony, and took another chocolate biscuit and chewed it absent-mindedly. "Are you going to tell me exactly how Alan Kirby met his death?"

"Yes, I'll come to that in due course. What I want you to tell me now is something about these three men of yours. What they do, what they're like, and have they the qualifications to be the organiser?"

"I'll start with Daniel Kirby, because he's by far the most likely. In fact it was his relationship to Alan that first aroused my interest. He's a big man, retired, and obviously very wealthy. A very forceful personality. And I don't think his relationship with his wife is one that would have interfered with some extra-marital fun and games with Louise Chorley. Neither of them seemed to care much for the other, though she took the trouble when she saw us out to tell us that Dan didn't mean all he said. But I think that was more because he showed a tendency to be down on Alan, whereas she is – was – very much on his side."

"And the other part of the question?" queried Sykes.

"Oh yes, on that score he's the most likely too. I think I can quote to you the exact words that were used to me about him: he is said to have the best private collection of art in Britain, if you exclude the Royal collections."

"When you say art, we're back to paintings, are we?"

"Yes."

"Where are they housed, I wonder."

"I'm not an expert, but I imagine that everything I saw was genuine. Certainly the furnishings were all antiques. But the Kirbys live in what's practically a mansion, and there are only the two of them, no children. So I imagine he has no difficulty in taking two or even three rooms as galleries." He stopped suddenly as a thought struck him. "Well," he added doubtfully, "perhaps I'm all wrong about him. But I think you'll agree he has to be considered."

"You say he was on bad terms with his nephew?"

"No, I didn't say that. He was inclined to think Alan was guilty, and rather impatient with him because he didn't share his uncle's taste. But then neither does Mrs Kirby, she told me that herself."

"Let's go on to the next member of the trio," Sykes suggested.

"That will be Raymond Shields, taking them in the order in which Geoffrey and I went to see them. He owns Holiday Press, and while there weren't the signs of great wealth that there were at the Kirbys' house, he and his wife certainly know how to make themselves comfortable. As you know, I suppose, Alan Kirby was one of his editors, particularly concerned with anything remotely connected with history, which was his subject. Shields was also Louise Chorley's publisher, and his wife, Constance, is Mrs Hilda Kirby's cousin. So he knew Alan quite well, and had actually visited him at his rooms on the Saturday morning before the painting was found there, to discuss a book they were thinking of publishing, about which there seemed to be some urgency. He was doubtful about Alan's innocence, because he knew how he disliked having a job, instead of being able to immerse himself in research work and write. He thought young Kirby would have taken any opportunity for making some extra money that would enable him to do that. His wife on the other hand, like Hilda Kirby, was all on Alan's side. Though now I come to think of it Hilda's position was really more that whatever he'd done it was all right with her."

"On the possibility of Shields being Louise Chorley's lover—"

"That's a difficult question to answer. Daniel Kirby's certainly the most personable of the three men, but then one can never understand other people's taste in these matters. There didn't seem to be any conflict between him and his wife, but Constance Shields did show a rather patronising attitude towards Mrs Chorley, almost bordering on dislike. That might or might not be significant."

"And the most important question, his knowledge of art?"

"If he liked Louise Chorley's stuff enough to publish it," said Antony a little tartly, "I imagine his taste is a zero quality. He also puts out greeting cards for all occasions, and I don't suppose that qualifies him as an art expert either. However, I have to add that Constance Shields, though she says she's only an amateur, must actually have a very comprehensive knowledge of the subject. For instance, she catalogued Daniel Kirby's collection for him, and now keeps the catalogue up to date . . . a labour of love, her husband said, by which I only mean she didn't get paid for it. And I can't see Daniel letting anyone near his precious things who didn't know how to value them."

"You think if Shields was the organiser . . . I'm getting tired of that word," said Sykes fretfully.

"I am myself, in fact I went so far as to use spider instead," Antony admitted. "If you're trying to ask me if I think his wife might have been an accomplice, I just don't know. I'm inclined to think not."

"Why is that?"

"Her attitude towards Louise might have been because she knew of some liaison between Mrs Chorley and her husband. If that was so she certainly wouldn't have collaborated with him."

"Then that rules him out right away."

"Not necessarily. I think he might be quite clever enough to get all the information he needed from her, about famous paintings and where they were housed, and about who among the collectors specialised in what."

"Some thefts have been of paintings that were on sale, like the Rubens from the Sefton Gallery that Alan Kirby was accused of having received," said Sykes. "And some have been from municipal collections, and some even from stately homes that are open to the public."

"That information, too, he could have found out from his wife. But here's a question for you, Chief Inspector. Have there been any thefts since Louise Chorley gave herself up to the police for the murder of her husband?"

90

"Two or three, the Rubens included. And that's a right puzzle, if your position is the correct one. Your spider was presumably in this for money; is it likely that he wanted Alan Kirby out of the way so badly that he'd forgo his profit?"

"The question of profit would only arise if he had a customer lined up for the painting," Antony pointed out. "It might have been a special effort, just for the purpose of discrediting Alan."

"Ah, so it might," said Sykes. "I don't know about you, lad, but it all seems a proper muddle to me."

"Then let me tell you about the last of my three men, Ernest Connolly. He's an editor on *The Courier*, and has a wife and four children, and they've just moved to a medium-priced house in North London, so recently that the garden isn't yet made. He'd visited Alan Kirby's rooms, some weeks before the incident we're talking about, to talk about a series of articles for the paper. That's really the best reason I have for putting him on the list."

"Did he also know Louise Chorley?"

"Yes, he did, partly because her poems used to appear first in *The Courier*, and he would use them as a stopgap when there was a space that needed filling; but even more because his wife was a genuine admirer of her work."

"So is mine," said Sykes gloomily.

"Well, there's a bond there. As for the likelihood of an affaire going on, I don't imagine Maria Connolly and Ernest have much in common, except perhaps the children, though I didn't see much sign of paternal love on his part. He says he has a catholic taste in paintings, but not the money to indulge it. Which perhaps is just as well, as he admitted himself, because his wife just thinks of paintings as dust traps, something else to complicate the cleaning of the house."

"Do you think his interest is genuine, or was he just trying to sound cultured? Some people do, you know."

"Yes, I'm aware of it. No, I think he's quite genuine about his love of paintings, at least there was an illustrated book on the paintings of Corot open on his sofa. The knowledge we're postulating for this organiser isn't unobtainable you know, and one thing you can say about working for a newspaper, one must acquire a wide circle of acquaintances. In fact, as far as I remember, he said as much to me."

"And that's all you can give me, Mr Maitland?"

"It is." Antony smiled at him. "I'm being remarkably communicative this morning, don't you think?"

"Remarkably." Sykes's tone was a little dry. "There's one thing you haven't told me, though. What sort of a description did you get from old Mr Brewster about the man he alleges to have seen importing the canvas into Mrs Campbell's house?"

"Unfortunately we didn't get any sort of a description at all. What happened was that he had a sort of flash of lucidity, when he told us about the man, but then he was completely vague by the time we asked him what he was like. He did use the word middling, but I don't think you could rely on that. He mentioned he wore a hat and raincoat, because it was drizzling that day; and he mentioned that Alan Kirby had gone out five minutes before. When we checked with him . . . I think I told you this already, Chief Inspector. It seemed that the day must have been the Sunday before the police arrived."

"Then I think," said Sykes, "we'll have another cup of coffee to celebrate your frankness." He turned and signalled to the waitress.

"I want Alan Kirby's murderer caught," said Maitland. His voice shook a little on the words, and the detective looked at him curiously.

"Yes, you've taken it to heart, haven't you?" he enquired. "Blaming yourself too, I shouldn't wonder." The waitress arrived then with the coffee pot, and there was a silence while the cups were replenished. When she had gone away again Sykes reached for the sugar basin, and added, "Well, you suggested this meeting, Mr Maitland, and I must admit you've performed your part of the bargain handsomely. What is it you want to know?"

"First of all, exactly what happened to Alan Kirby?"

"He was shot down in the street. On his way home, I suppose, as Mrs Campbell told me later that he'd been out most of the day."

92

"Yes, I understood that from what Geoffrey told me. Wasn't anybody about?"

"Oh yes, several people, and as usual their evidence is completely contradictory. It all happened so quickly," said Sykes in what was evidently intended to be an echo of what he had been told.

"They must have seen something," Antony protested.

"A dark car, medium sized. Each one had a different maker's name for it."

"I see. There's one thing that has occurred to me, Chief Inspector; there must have been a lot of cars parked in the street. How was the gunman able to take aim at him?"

"That's one thing the witnesses were unanimous about," said Sykes. "The car was double parked near the turning from the Earls Court Road. One of them noticed that the driver was sitting in it, and when Kirby wanted to cross and came out between two parked cars he started up immediately. Kirby waited, of course, for the car to pass him, but instead of that it halted long enough for the driver to take aim and fire. As far as the doctors could tell, he was killed instantly."

Maitland was silent for a moment, obviously brooding. "I was wondering you see, whether there was just one man concerned, or whether it was more like a gang killing."

"Just one man, I think," said Sykes cautiously. "Driving away from Earls Court Road, he was on the left, of course, and Kirby was crossing from the right. It's just possible that there might have been a second man in the back of the car. Would that make any great difference?"

"It's a question of how this organiser of yours works," said Antony. "I got the impression from what you've told me about Nobby Clark and the modern painting that perhaps he worked alone, unknown to any of the people he employed."

"Yes, I see what you mean. I can only tell you my own feeling, Mr Maitland, that the man works alone. In this case a shotgun was used, the street isn't very wide, as you know, and the mess was considerable."

Maitland looked at him coldly. "I've already told you all I can," he said, "so you needn't bother to try to fan the flames of my anger."

93

"There's just one thing," said Sykes, letting the remark slide past him without comment. "Did you discover anyone who might have had a grudge against your client? That might be a material point."

"I could find no smell of a motive for anyone wanting to frame him, still less for wanting him dead," said Maitland firmly. "I can't help you, Chief Inspector. I would if I could but I can't. But I'm firmly convinced – don't tell me it isn't logical – that this whole business is somehow tied in with the ring of art thieves, and with the man Louise Chorley said was her lover, whom she was trying to protect when she shot her husband."

"Yes, I was already aware of your opinions," said Sykes, amused. He had been stirring carefully the five lumps of sugar he had added to his coffee, but now he put down the spoon in the saucer and took a sip. "Is that all you wanted to know?" he asked. "About Alan Kirby's death?"

"Just one more question," said Antony. "Since the events of last March, have the police been doing anything to try to find Louise Chorley's lover?"

"Of course we have. Not the murder squad of course, the people who are concerned with the art thefts."

"Well?"

"Well what, Mr Maitland?" said Sykes innocently.

"You can't leave it there," Antony protested. "I want to know what you found out."

"Yes, I was afraid of that. The answer is, if you'll pardon the expression, Mr Maitland," said Sykes unnecessarily, "damn all."

"She never gave you the slightest hint of his identity?"

"All we have is her original statement. She mentioned the fact to explain the shooting of her husband, she was afraid he might give her lover away. After that we couldn't get a word out of her, and, of course, since her arrest there's been no question of asking her again. There was also the story she wrote, and sold to *The Courier* in return for their paying her legal expenses. She had no objection at all to our seeing that, in spite of her solicitor's misgivings, but it didn't give us any more information."

"Poor old Bellerby. What a woman to have to deal with."

"Yes, I imagine he finds her very trying. However, I don't see any possibility of this statement, this article, whatever you like to call it, being admitted at the trial."

"But surely there must have been some hint, if she'd been seeing this man regularly."

"All I can say is, they must have been extraordinarily discreet. She met Shields from time to time, of course, in his capacity as her publisher, and Connolly too because of her connection with *The Courier*. The Kirbys were both close friends. But we found no suggestion at all that there had been any – shall we say illicit? – meetings."

"You're confining yourself to my three names. Was there no suggestion of her being involved with anybody else?"

"Only the group you investigated when Sir Nicholas was defending Mrs Selden," said Sykes. "And quite frankly, from that point of view, I'd be inclined to say their lives were an open book."

"Yes, I think so too. I wonder... do you think she feels at all depressed because this man hasn't offered to pay for her defence?"

"If she does it's pretty unreasonable of her. How could he come forward without admitting what he'd been up to? And you must remember, Mr Maitland, I haven't seen the lady since the day she was arrested."

"No. It's a bit disappointing though."

"What are you going to do now?" asked Sykes, stirring his coffee again unnecessarily.

"I don't know what I *can* do, except struggle with a feeling of guilt," said Antony, speaking of his feelings with unusual honesty. "Uncle Nick pointed out, as you did, that I'd no shadow of an excuse for asking any further questions of anybody. Anyway, you've got the matter in hand."

"You aren't always so willing to leave things to us, Mr Maitland," Sykes pointed out, again with the amused look which he so often wore when they met.

"I don't think I have much choice," said Antony smiling. "But I think... oh, I feel it in my bones that one of those three is your master mind. Though what Louise Chorley saw in any one of them," he added grumpily, "I can't imagine."

*

95

He got back to chambers and found Sir Nicholas alone in his room. "Now I wonder," said counsel, taking off his spectacles and giving his nephew a keen look, "exactly where you've been this morning."

"How did you know I'd been out?"

"I happened to overhear Willett telephoning to postpone a conference on your behalf. I can't remember you ever doing anything like that before, Antony, however serious things might seem."

"This is . . . different."

"Oh, for heaven's sake, use your head my dear boy. You can't hold yourself responsible—"

"Can't I?" asked Antony quizzically.

"Well, being you I suppose you can. I also suppose that it was something to do with Alan Kirby's murder with which you were concerning yourself."

"If you must know, I was talking to Sykes."

"At your request or at his?" asked Sir Nicholas sharply.

"At my suggestion. Alan was gunned down with a shotgun. Sykes thinks there was only the driver in the car, which paused for a moment while he took aim; but he isn't absolutely certain there might not have been another man in the back."

"And what use is that information to you, I wonder?"

"I'm only trying to get some ideas of the way this organiser operates," Antony explained. "I think he's extremely cautious, and even his henchmen don't know who he is."

"David Chorley certainly knew, or why should Louise have shot him?"

"There's that, of course, but I suppose he was a special case. Anyway I may be all wrong about it and it doesn't seem to matter. The police have had no luck in discovering who Mrs Chorley's lover was, and I don't see how I can succeed where they've failed."

"You're assuming that the same person who organised the art thefts killed Alan Kirby," said Sir Nicholas. "You know, Antony, I think that's a pretty wild guess, even for you."

"It's a gut feeling," said Antony bluntly, and ignored his

96

uncle's pained look. "Anyway, as I said, there's nothing more I can do. Does that satisfy you?"

"Is that all that passed between you and Sykes?"

"He wanted to know what Geoffrey's and my enquiries had uncovered, and I gave him the full story. For all the good it will be to him, any more than it is to me."

"Nothing more?"

"We drank two cups of coffee together, and we had some chocolate biscuits," said Antony precisely. "I told him about Mr Brewster too, but there's nothing in that. Sykes pointed out, quite correctly, all the things that the theory of Alan Kirby's innocence would leave unexplained."

"And I was just about to suggest that we go to lunch together. One long round of pleasure," said Sir Nicholas sardonically.

"If you call talking to the police pleasure, I don't," said Antony emphatically.

"No, I think you're quite aware of my opinion on *that* subject," his uncle told him. "However, if you'll sit down for a moment there's something I should like to discuss with you before we go. How do you feel about doing a favour for a friend of mine?"

"What sort of a favour?" asked Maitland cautiously.

"A professional one," said Sir Nicholas blandly.

"Who for?"

"Halloran."

"He hasn't much time for me," said Antony bluntly.

"On the contrary, I know for a fact that he has the greatest respect for your abilities. He's also pretty confident of his own ability to control your more extravagant ideas, when you're working in association with him."

"You're trying to tell me he wants my help with a case. I've enough on my mind already."

"This is something you may find . . . not uninteresting," Sir Nicholas told him. "You know – I told you myself – that he's prosecuting Louise Chorley. Unfortunately Carrington, who was acting as his junior, is in hospital with a ruptured appendix; and as the trial is expected to come on not later than the beginning of next week –"

"I'm not touting for work, Uncle Nick."

"No, I took the opportunity of your absence this morning

to go over your list with Mallory. It's comfortably full, but with a little rearrangement—"

"And whose suggestion was this, yours or Halloran's?"

"He happened to mention to me," said Sir Nicholas, lying blandly, "the difficulty in which he found himself. I admit that, seeing how worried he was, I did bring up your name."

Antony laughed suddenly. "I bet you did!" he said. "You know perfectly well, Uncle Nick, that I acted with Halloran for the prosecution once many years ago, and he didn't like my efforts one little bit."

"I dare say he's forgiven you by this time," said Sir Nicholas equably.

"I wonder."

"I think you'll find he's willing to let bygones be bygones. So long as you don't attempt anything similar on this occasion."

"I've no interest in Louise Chorley's fate. But it would be rather amusing," he added reflectively, "to come up against Kevin O'Brien again, as opponents this time."

"Then you'll go and see Halloran this afternoon?" Sir Nicholas urged him.

"If you like," said Antony, rather reluctantly.

"For heaven's sake!" Sir Nicholas was impatient. "I thought you wanted the opportunity of cross-examining these people you say have been called as character witnesses."

"I did, I do, though I don't know how you guessed it. And thinking it over, you know, I don't see that there's the faintest chance of getting anything out of them."

"Then that is one thing we can agree upon," said Sir Nicholas cordially. "You'll find Halloran in chambers at three o'clock this afternoon, and meanwhile may I suggest that we follow my original plan and get some lunch?"

Bruce Halloran was a big, heavy man, very dark of complexion – though his black hair was showing signs of greying now – so that in court the gleaming white of his wig and bands made a somewhat startling contrast. He had a deep voice, rather too loud and booming unless he remembered to modulate it, when Maitland had been known to say of him disrespectfully that he could coo you like any sucking dove. It was well hidden, but he had a certain affection for his younger colleague, who had been outrageously rude to him in court the first time they had encountered each other. But this affection, of course, was without prejudice to his feeling free to express himself on the other man's shortcomings whenever he felt so inclined. Now he lumbered to his feet when Maitland was shown into his room, waited carefully until the door was shut behind him, and then remarked, not without a tinge of sarcasm in his tone, "I never thought Harding would bring you up to the starting post, Maitland."

"Well, here I am," said Antony mildly. He was only too well aware that Halloran was trying to bait him, and that any loss of temper on his part – which was dangerously near – would have merely caused the other man a certain sardonic amusement. "Uncle Nick tells me I'm in a position to do you a favour," he said, and his voice too held a note of satire.

Halloran grinned at that and flung himself back in his chair, which trembled under the onslaught but resisted the temptation to crumple to pieces to the floor. "Sit down, sit down," he said, waving his hand invitingly. "Yes, Maitland, I should be very much obliged if you would consent to act with me in this matter of Louise Chorley."

"I shall be happy to," said Antony, equally formally.

"I can see Harding's point, of course." For the moment Halloran seemed to have decided to play the scene perfectly straight. "You're well aware of all the circumstances, in fact you might almost say you drove her to do what she did."

"There's not a soul knows about that, outside the circle of people who were in the Walpoles' set. And for obvious reasons I imagine you won't be calling any of them."

"It would be in the worst of taste," Halloran agreed solemnly. "However, I think I'm entitled to know what kind of a stunt you intend to pull this time," he added, suddenly abandoning cover and coming out into the open.

"Stunt?" said Antony, as guilelessly as he could. "What makes you think–?"

"Harding filled me in. It seems you're upset over the death of a client of yours, and think that one of the defence witnesses in this case might be the man who killed him. There's one thing he didn't mention though, and I must admit I'd like to know the answer. How did you come to connect Alan Kirby with Mrs Chorley?"

"That's something I'm afraid I can't tell you." He had had a talk over the telephone with Kevin O'Brien before he came round to Halloran's chambers, explaining the position, and had assured him of his silence about their previous discussion. Luckily Kevin trusted him now; at an earlier stage in their acquaintance it might have been different.

"Not even now we're colleagues?" Halloran insisted.

"Not even now, I'm sorry. Is there anything else—?"

"Not at the moment. Except that I want it clearly understood, Antony," said Halloran, who rarely deviated from the customary use of his fellow barristers' surnames, "that if this idea of yours interferes in any way with the job we're trying to do, you forget about it on the instant."

"Yes, I understand that," said Maitland, relaxing a little. "Can you put me in the picture?"

Halloran came to his feet, tugged at his lapels, and took a turn or two about the room. Antony, always restless himself in times of stress, would have been glad enough to follow his example, but there certainly wasn't room for two of them to be prowling about. "In one way it's a simple case," said Halloran, "because we have her confession. It's true she'll be pleading Not Guilty by reason of insanity, but that leaves the onus of proof on the defence. Our side of it will be simple. I propose to begin with the police evidence of the fact that David Chorley was about to be arrested for murder, and that his motive for that murder arose from the art thefts that have been occurring in such great quantity lately. Detective Chief Inspector Sykes can handle most of it, though there'll be the person who received her call at the police station as well, and a ballistics expert, of course. After that the medical evidence concerning Chorley's death, and then a psychiatrist or two who'll echo our point of view, that she's perfectly sane."

"And you're hoping to get her confession included in Sykes's evidence? Do you think that'll be possible?"

"Yes, I think so, in fact I'm sure of it. You see, Kevin O'Brien intends to base his defence on that article she wrote for *The Courier*. They can't reproduce it while the case is still *sub judice*, but there's nothing to stop the defence doing so."

"I don't quite see—" He wondered as he spoke if he was overdoing it, but there was no point in making Halloran as wise as himself concerning his original talk with Kevin.

"It's quite simple. The whole thing was a delusion on her part," said Halloran airily, "pure imagination. So it's obvious that she's mad."

"It wasn't obvious to me when I met her."

"No, but you know as well as I do that's nothing to do with it. If O'Brien can convince the jury—"

"Do *you* think she's insane?" asked Antony.

"No, I don't. If I did I'd have taken steps to see that she was pronounced unfit to plead. But in my view her place is in prison, not in an institution where some fool of a doctor may release her on an unsuspecting world after a year or two."

That was an exact echo of Maitland's own thoughts on the subject, so he had no quarrel with it. "Do you think O'Brien can prove his point?" he asked curiously.

"That depends. In part it depends, I suppose, on whether I can rely on you."

"As a matter of fact, you can."

Halloran looked at him hard for a moment. "Yes, I think you mean that," he said. "Only I'm not happy with this secondary motive of yours, and I can't say I am."

"I agree with you there too," said Antony, rather ruefully.

"One of your damned crusades," growled Halloran. It was Geoffrey Horton who had first coined that phrase, but Halloran was famous for knowing everything that went on in his own restricted legal world.

"I'm afraid it is," said Maitland apologetically.

"Well," said Halloran, suddenly brisk, "I'll get Carrington's chambers to send the papers round to you as soon as

101

possible. Do you think you can be ready by the end of the week?"

"If I must."

"It may not come on till Monday, but I know it's near the head of the list. That would give you a bit more time, wouldn't it?"

"It would indeed."

"In any case we'll have another conference – Thursday perhaps? – when you've had time to look into things."

So they left the matter there, each reasonably satisfied with the arrangement, though each of them would have admitted to some uneasiness too. The Thursday conference dragged on for nearly three hours, and Maitland, leaving and walking across to his uncle's chambers again, felt – the idea had occurred to him before – how much time could be wasted in a matter like this on nothing but talk. On the other hand there were certainly occasions when personal contact was the only way to get anything done; this just didn't happen to be one of them.

Sykes phoned him that night, and the undercurrent of amusement in his voice was very clear. "I hear you've accepted a brief in the Chorley case," he said, after the usual enquiries had been decorously completed.

"To help Bruce Halloran out, he's a friend of my uncle's, you know that."

"I shall be giving evidence for the prosecution."

"I know that too."

"Yes, I suppose you do. I shall have to explain to the court how it came about that we were on the point of arresting David Chorley. Suppose I tell them that was all your doing?"

"You wouldn't do that," said Maitland quickly, before he realised that the detective, in the straight-faced way of some north-countrymen, was pulling his leg. "Well, of course I know you wouldn't," he added, "it isn't relevant at all."

"It seems a pity," said Sykes, still solemn, "not to give credit where credit is due."

"That's a kind thought, but on the whole I think I'm happier with things as they are," said Antony, entering

102

into the spirit of the thing. "Was that why you called me, Chief Inspector?"

"I'm curious," Sykes admitted.

"What about?"

"About what you think you're going to get out of all this," said Sykes. "It doesn't seem to me—"

"If you want the whole truth, Chief Inspector, it doesn't seem to me either," said Antony. "But it's my only hope now of getting near the people who knew Louise Chorley."

"If we're both right in thinking that this spider of yours is a loner," said Sykes, suddenly genuinely serious, "he may have nothing to do with Alan Kirby—"

"I don't like coincidences," Antony put in.

" — either by framing him, as you think," Sykes continued, not to be put off his stroke, "or by killing him. And in that case, Mr Maitland, I hope you realise that the organiser might be anybody in the whole world."

As a matter of form Antony protested that this was too sweeping a statement, but he couldn't get it altogether out of his mind, and carried it to bed with him that night. For that matter, it stayed with him over the weekend, as the case of Regina *versus* Chorley wasn't called until the following Monday.

PART II

REGINA *VERSUS* CHORLEY, 1972

THE CASE FOR THE PROSECUTION

Monday, the first day of the trial

Maitland sometimes thought that Mr Justice Carruthers would never grow old. It was a long time now since they had first encountered each other in court, and the judge didn't look a day older and was still as spry as ever. He was a small man, with a face rather like a bloodhound . . . an intelligent one, Maitland thought, but that – though not altogether respectful – was because over the years a certain understanding had grown up between the two men. Maitland, for his part, knew Carruthers to be fair, as far as is possible for anyone in this imperfect world. He might not always like the judge's decisions, but they would be based on the facts as they had been presented in court.

Carruthers, in his turn, did not disapprove, as so many of his brethren did, of Maitland's unorthodox ways. In fact he was amused by them, and had found them often a leaven to the boredom of some particularly dull matter. This morning he was intrigued to find Antony appearing for the prosecution. It wasn't the first time he'd worked with Bruce Halloran, though the previous occasions had mostly been when he was much younger, and still at the junior bar. This case was an important one, certainly, and it wasn't at all out of the way for two Queen's Counsel to be appearing for the prosecution; what was odd was to find Maitland not in the defence team. That was his proper place, that was where the judge would have expected to find him, and Mr Justice Carruthers looked forward to seeing what the change portended.

Halloran, of course, he also knew well: there would be no surprises there. A big man with a big voice who would make each point clearly, and who had the unexpected knack of cross-examining a witness almost savagely, without antagonising the jury. Neither were there any surprises in the defence team. Kevin O'Brien was a battler, and an espouser of lost causes, which somehow in his capable hands very often turned out not to be lost at all. His junior, Derek Stringer, was from Sir Nicholas's chambers, and a good friend, as Carruthers knew, of Maitland, with whom he had often worked. Whoever had made the choice of teaming him with O'Brien, it had been a good one; he was capable of a down-to-earth approach (which had often served him well when working with the more volatile Maitland) and should be capable, if anybody could, of curbing O'Brien's wilder flights of fancy. He was a very tall man, prematurely bald, who assumed a hairpiece when he took off his wig in the robing-room. Carruthers found it easy enough to forgive him this small vanity; Stringer had, the judge remembered, a very beautiful wife, and somehow the two facts linked together in his mind.

And now that he remembered it, the judge thought, the last time they had appeared before him O'Brien and Maitland had been in a way teamed together; each had a separate client, but the two were jointly accused of murder. This case at least would form a complete contrast.

While these thoughts were passing through his head the indictment was being read, and he turned his attention now to the defendant. Louise Chorley was tall for a woman, probably about five foot six or seven, and she was standing quietly with a vacant look on her face which seemed to suggest that she was quite impervious to all that was going on around her. She was very thin, with a patrician cast of countenance, though rather haggard looking, and with a stringy neck. She also had very fine brown hair that fell in wisps about her face, and what Mr Justice Carruthers considered in his old-fashioned way to be a Bohemian way of dressing. That is, she was wearing a long, loose garment that the judge vaguely classed in his mind as Indian, and a great many strings of beads. Altogether, a colourful costume. And I shouldn't think, said Carruthers to himself, that she ever wore a hat in her life until today; but somebody had persuaded her to balance a sort of cap on her head – the least common denominator of a hat, perhaps – where it perched, supremely incongruous.

When the time came she pleaded Not Guilty, but her counsel had to prompt her before she answered the question at all. Then it was the judge's turn. "I'm sure, Madam, you would be more comfortable if you were seated," he suggested, and had to repeat the remark twice before one of the wardesses came forward to guide the prisoner to the chair that had been placed for her in the dock. All throughout Halloran's opening remarks, which were brief, she maintained the same aloof air; apparently not hearing what was being said, or – if she heard – neither understanding nor caring.

Maitland was observing all this with a sardonic eye. So she was all set to play up the by-reason-of-insanity angle for all she was worth, was she? Not that anything was changed in her appearance – except the hat – though as he remembered it there had been before an intense look in her eyes, rather at variance with her otherwise droopy look. According to his information, O'Brien intended to call her in her own defence, and it would be interesting to see how she acted then. Meanwhile, here was the police sergeant who had been on duty when Louise Chorley's telephone call came in, to describe her announcement that she had just shot her husband. At any other time Antony would have listened with interest to Bruce Halloran's expert handling of the witness, but this was an old story to him, and he had his own preoccupation with his plans. But that was for later.

The sergeant was followed by the constable who had been first on the scene, and then by a plain-clothes man who identified himself as a ballistics expert and described in rather boring detail – as if anyone were denying it – the points that made it certain that the gun found in the same room as the body had been the one with which David Chorley was shot. After that, another detective. This one's job was finger-prints, and Louise Chorley had apparently made no attempt to wipe hers from the weapon. As, indeed, why should she when she was about to confess?

By that time it was Chief Inspector Sykes's turn to appear in the witness-box, and everybody perked up a little, hoping for matters of greater interest. Halloran was suave with him. "I think it would be best if you were to tell us

109

about all this in your own words, Inspector," he suggested when the preliminaries were over.

That was a good move, Maitland thought. Sykes was a solid-looking citizen, who would be bound to impress the jury. "To explain my rather premature arrival on the scene, sir," said the detective, "it will be necessary for me to go back a little."

"We shall be interested to hear what you have to say, Chief Inspector," said Halloran, not to be outdone in politeness.

Sykes, thank goodness, wasn't one of the acting-on-information-received brigade. "I have to refer to a crime which is no part of this enquiry," he said. "A woman named Emily Walpole had been murdered, and our enquiries into her death had led us to interview David Chorley, the husband of the defendant in this case. What he told us prompted us to apply for a warrant for his arrest. I arrived back at the house with Detective Inspector Mayhew to find the suspect already dead, and Constable Barton in attendance, in consequence of the accused's telephone call. I may add that David Chorley had left a confession of his guilt in the matter of Emily Walpole's death."

"Thank you, Chief Inspector." He waited a moment, not so much to allow the buzz of interest among the spectators to subside, but until the usher's cries for silence were finished. "Can you tell us now, had your enquiries revealed any motive for this murder?"

"Yes, Mrs Walpole was an art expert, a partner in the firm of Verlaine and Walpole. She had seen a certain picture in Mr Chorley's possession, which only later did she realise had been stolen. Being a friend of his, she was reluctant to believe that he had received it in this knowledge, and made it her business to ask him where he had acquired it." He looked up for a moment at the judge. "I'm trying to explain things, my lord, without going into controversial matters. It is believed that David Chorley agreed to explain matters to Mrs Walpole the following evening, and so had the opportunity to kill her."

"You say he had written a confession?"

"Yes indeed, though only the bare fact that he was guilty."

"Then I think we may go on to what you found when you arrived at the Chorleys' residence on the day of David Chorley's death. You say you found Constable Barton there. Who else was present?"

"Only the accused, Mrs Louise Chorley."

Carruthers sat back again, and waved a hand in what Halloran took to be permission to return to his witness. "Constable Barton has told us she was in a state of great agitation when he arrived," he said.

"There was no sign of that by the time I got there, rather I should say she seemed numb. In consequence of what Barton told me I suggested that she should call her solicitor. This she refused, and insisted upon making an immediate statement."

Here Mr Justice Carruthers leaned forward again. "Mr Halloran," he said.

"M'lud?"

"Are you proposing to put this statement into evidence?"

"I was just about to do so, M'lud."

"What have you to say to that, Mr O'Brien?"

Kevin O'Brien came to his feet. "That I haven't the slightest objection in the world, my lord," he said cheerfully, and just for the moment the hint of brogue in his voice – which Antony knew perfectly well was completely spurious – was very marked.

Carruthers frowned at him. "Are you familiar with the contents of Mrs Chorley's statement?" he asked.

"Certainly I am, my lord. Perhaps it will set your lordship's mind at rest if I tell you that if my learned friend had not introduced this statement into evidence, I should myself have done so."

Carruthers sat back again. "You know your own business best, Mr O'Brien," he said doubtfully. "Very well, Mr Halloran, you may proceed."

The statement was produced, the formality of placing it in evidence complied with. "Perhaps now, Chief Inspector, you would read us what it says," said Halloran. "As you know well enough, it's an important document in this

111

case, so take it slowly so that we all have time to understand its content." Maitland suppressed a smile at that; he knew well enough that his leader meant, so that the jury have time. They shared the belief, common to most lawyers, that the collective intelligence of any given jury is not very high. This one consisted of seven men, and five women, of whom some looked self-important and some plain scared. A fair-to-average bunch on the whole.

Sykes cleared his throat. "This is the statement of Louise Chorley, as made to me, and recorded by Police Constable Barton, on the twenty-third of March, 1972. *I had known all along that David* – that's her husband," he interpolated – *"had been the one to kill Emily Walpole, though he never admitted as much to me until today. He had been concerned with the art thefts for some time, at my suggestion –"*

"One moment, Mr Sykes," said the judge. "Are we to understand that this statement was made as the result of some question and answer?"

"Yes indeed, my lord."

"Then did you ask her to explain that last statement?"

"I thought it best not to interrupt the flow of her narrative more than was necessary. As you will see, my lord, the matter explains itself a little later on."

"Thank you, Mr Sykes, you may continue."

"My reason for doing this – that is, making the suggestion, my lord – *was because I knew David to be a completely amoral man, and with a strong sense of adventure. Any enterprise of a risky nature would be bound to appeal to him. After the detectives had questioned him this morning* – that was myself, my lord, and Detective Inspector Mayhew – *in part in my presence, David was completely demoralised. I thought it very likely that his arrest would follow, and that if he were arrested he would make a complete statement of everything that had happened. That was unthinkable –"*

"Again I have to ask you, Mr Sykes, did you ask for an explanation of that remark?"

"The reason will appear, my lord." He looked down again at the papers in his hand, though it was obvious

112

enough to Maitland that he knew them pretty well by heart. *"That was unthinkable,"* he repeated, *"so I suggested to him that he write out a confession, just the bare fact that he had killed Emily Walpole, nothing else, and then refuse to answer any other questions. But I knew in my heart that he wouldn't be able to resist talking, and he was the only person, besides myself, to know who the organiser of the art thefts was. So I had already made up my mind what to do. David had always owned a gun. I don't know where it came from in the first place but that hardly seems to matter. While he was writing I fetched it, and when he had finished writing I shot him. That is all I have to say."*

"Mr Sykes, you told us – " began the judge.

"Indeed I did, your lordship. The statement continues," said Sykes prosaically.

"In answer to your questions?"

"Not altogether. I think she felt I wouldn't believe her, unless she explained her reasons. But first she said, *I've never used a gun before, it took two shots before I was sure he was dead. I had to do it, you see, I had to do it, because otherwise he'd have told you everything and I couldn't have that. The man who was organising the thefts, to whom I suggested David's name as an assistant, has been my lover for many years. That's a dreadful thing to say, isn't it, Chief Inspector?"* Sykes went on in an unemotional tone, but Maitland could imagine the rather arch look that might have accompanied the words, *"a middle-aged housewife like myself. I've lost him now, of course, by this action, but at least he'll be safe."*

"Is that the end of the statement, Chief Inspector?" asked Halloran.

"Yes, that's everything," Sykes confirmed.

"Did you ask the lady the name of this man, this lover of hers?"

"I did, of course, but that was all she would say, just that he would be safe now."

"Then perhaps you'll continue with your narrative of events."

"Certainly I will. There was a gun on the table, a .38 revolver which Mrs Chorley identified as being the one she

113

had used, and which was subsequently tested by ballistics."

"We have already heard evidence on that point, Chief Inspector."

"In the circumstances," Skyes went on, completely unmoved by the interruption, "I suggested that we should adjourn to the police station, and again asked her to telephone her solicitor. Finally she agreed to this, and it was arranged that Mr Bellerby should meet us there. The formalities of her arrest were then completed, and I had no further opportunity to talk to her."

Halloran had a few more questions, bringing out one or two points more clearly, stressing that by the time Sykes arrived at the Chorleys' house the accused had been completely calm again. "That is all, Chief Inspector," he said at last and seated himself.

"Have you any questions, Mr O'Brien?" Carruthers asked.

"A few, my lord." Kevin was on his feet in an instant. "There are just two points I should like to bring up with you, Chief Inspector," he went on. "This so-called organiser of a series of art thefts, have you any proof of his existence?"

"All I can say, sir, is that there has been too much activity in that line for any other explanation to be possible."

"In other words, to paraphrase the well-known saying, if he didn't exist it would have been necessary for the police to invent him?"

"I think we have enough evidence of his existence," said Sykes stolidly.

"Any clue to his identity?"

"None at all."

"In spite of the fact that, I presume, extensive enquiries have been made?"

"This is not really my department, Mr O'Brien," said Sykes. Halloran came to his feet.

"The prosecution is quite willing to accept your evidence on this point, Chief Inspector," he said.

"Thank you." O'Brien gave a little bow in the direction

114

of Counsel for the Prosecution. "Extensive enquiries have been made?" he insisted.

"Indeed they have."

"One would think," said O'Brien casually, "that Mrs Chorley's statement had given you a new point of departure."

"Yes, it did. Our enquiries were concentrated, I suppose you might say, upon people known to her."

"And still with no results?"

"Unfortunately, no."

"In fact, though you feel you have evidence that such a person as the one you call the organiser exists, there is only Mrs Chorley's word for the fact he was ever her lover?"

"That is so."

"Then let us turn to the question of her confession. I agree it was circumstantial enough, but you must admit that an official statement, read in dry official tones, does not perhaps convey very well the emotions of its maker at the time."

"I agree about the dry official tones," said Sykes, something very near a smile lighting his solemnity. "And I'll agree with you, the statement was not made without emotion, but she was calm enough about the death of her husband, the thing that concerned her was the possible effect of recent events upon the man she loved."

"I put it to you, Chief Inspector, that we have no evidence at all that this man ever existed."

"Only Mrs Chorley's word," agreed Sykes stolidly.

And that, with a few minor variations, was the extent of O'Brien's cross-examination. When he sat down Mr Justice Carruthers took the immediate opportunity of adjourning for the luncheon recess.

After they reconvened came the medical evidence, and Maitland felt very much inclined to go to sleep. He knew perfectly well by this time how David Chorley had died. This was always the part of a brief that least appealed to him, though if he had been leading he would have felt bound to study it carefully. In the circumstances, with the facts not really under dispute, he had felt justified in skimming over it very quickly. In the event, he had no reason to regret it; Halloran had a very few questions to ask, for the purposes of clarity, and Kevin O'Brien didn't even bother to get to his feet. But when the usher called for Dr Gavin Macintyre, it wasn't only Maitland who pricked up his ears, the whole feeling in the court seemed to change to one of more immediate interest.

On Antony's part this was understandable enough, Dr Macintyre was a very old friend of his, whose evidence he had used on a number of occasions for the defence. In appearance, the witness might well have been chosen for a character part in a Scottish film: he was a tall, rangy man with a deep jaw and a laconic manner. He caught Maitland's eye as he put down the bible after taking the oath; his was expressionless, but Antony knew well enough what he was thinking. *This is all a lot of nonsense; whatever I may say, they can bring someone to refute it. How on earth is the jury to decide between us?* Well, that would have been a fair enough question, but they had to go through the motions.

This time Halloran, perhaps because he knew the two men were acquainted, left the questioning to Maitland. After taking the doctor through the preliminary questions, including one as to his qualifications, which were formidable, Antony asked, "I take it, Doctor, you have examined the accused lady, Mrs Louise Chorley."

"That's why I'm here," said Macintyre, neatly pointing out the obvious.

"Yes, of course. Where did this interview take place?"

"In the Women's Prison at Holloway. To be more exact, in a room adjoining the prison hospital. The matron was also present."

"And in spite of the fact that it was in no way a physical examination, I imagine that the consent of the accused had been obtained."

"It had." Macintyre was a little gruff over that, he was too old a fox to be taken in by such tricks. "I have her request for my attendance in writing, and I was accompanied by the divisional surgeon as is customary in these cases, though what help *his* opinion would be—"

"Thank you, Doctor," said Maitland quickly, before his witness could proceed too far with what was obviously

116

going to be an indiscretion. The old boy had been wise, he thought; English judges were inclined to differ as to the necessity for this consent being obtained, but he was pretty sure Carruthers wouldn't stand for any laxity on the subject. "You were examining the prisoner with a particular question in mind, were you not?" he went on.

"Whether or not she was insane," said Macintyre bluntly.

"Perhaps you would be kind enough to tell us how your talk with her progressed."

"We talked quietly for a little while, not at all about her predicament."

"She still showed no aversion to talking to you?"

"None at all. She seemed eager to do so."

"Do you mean, Doctor, that she showed some signs of excitement?"

"No, not that. She was, throughout, extraordinarily calm. The only emotion she showed was when she spoke of a man whom she referred to throughout as her beloved."

"You have answered my question, Doctor, but I think I led you a little out of line. We'd better take all this in chronological order."

"Very well." Macintyre had at the best of times a dry way of speaking, and in the witness stand this seemed to be intensified. "I said we talked on neutral subjects, she showed me some of her poems, she seemed very proud of them. I don't say they were exactly to my taste, and I'm not a sentimental man, but I can see that by certain people they might be well received."

"I believe that to be the case," said Maitland gravely. "You would not, I take it, regard a liking for such things as a sign of insanity."

"Certainly not!"

Maitland glanced at O'Brien to see how he took that rather vehement statement. Counsel for the Defence was smiling to himself, and Derek Stringer was scribbling industriously. "And Mrs Chorley's manner throughout this part of the conversation was perfectly calm?" he said.

"Perfectly calm. When we had been talking along these lines for a little while, and felt comfortable together, I

117

asked her how it came about that she was in prison, awaiting trial."

"What did she say to that?"

"She said, *I shot my husband.* She said it quite simply, as though it was the most natural thing in the world. So, of course, I asked her why."

"And what reply did you get to that?"

"She said – I'll try to repeat her words exactly – she said, *He was a man who didn't know when to keep his mouth shut.* Naturally I asked her what she meant by that statement and she said it had been in his power to hurt someone she loved very much. She said, as I think I told you, her beloved, and the times when she spoke of him were the only times she showed any emotion at all."

"Just a minute, Doctor. You don't suppose it could have been a woman she was referring to?"

"Louise Chorley is not a lesbian," said Macintyre flatly. "Apart from my own observation – and I'm not without experience, as you were at pains to demonstrate at the beginning of my evidence, Mr Maitland – I'm in no doubt about that at all. If my opinion requires any confirmation, I may say that she referred to this person throughout as He or Him. A woman with lesbian tendencies would never have done that."

"I only wondered," said Maitland meekly. "Did she tell you how long this affaire of hers had been going on?"

"Not exactly. I must admit that she spoke as if it were eternal, no beginning, no end."

"And she never told you the man's name?"

"No. I queried her on the subject, but she refused to answer."

"That, of course, is completely consistent with the reason she gave for shooting her husband."

"Anything else would have been illogical," Macintyre agreed.

"I have to put the question to you bluntly, Doctor. Do you consider the accused, Mrs Louise Chorley, to be sane?"

"I do."

"And at the time she killed her husband, did she know exactly what she was doing?"

"To my mind, undoubtedly."

"Thank you, Doctor." Antony sat down again, and for once in his life was greeted by Halloran with a grunt of approval. Kevin O'Brien was already on his feet.

"Now, Doctor Macintyre," he said, "may I ask you how long your examination of my client took?"

"I was with her for over two hours."

"From what has just passed between you and my learned friend, it doesn't sound as if the conversation could have taken so long."

"There was a good deal of repetition, not unnaturally. We went over the same points again and again. I imagine," said Macintyre, suddenly carrying the game into the prosecution's own court, "that your learned friend felt that one repetition was sufficient for the jury."

"Yes, I'm sure he did," said O'Brien, completely unruffled. "And I promise my questions to you will be brief enough not to weary them, Doctor. In fact there is in essence only one question I wish to ask you. This so-called lover of Mrs Chorley's, have you any proof that he exists?"

"Proof? Proof isn't my business except as concerns my own profession," said the doctor unanswerably. "I have the lady's word for it, however."

"But you said she was emotional when she spoke of him. Their love was eternal," said O'Brien, quoting, "and had no beginning and no end. Would you say that was altogether a rational remark?"

"I should say she was quite clearly obsessed with her love for him."

"Might she not have imagined his existence?"

"It's a possibility I considered, of course. I decided against it."

"And apart from this obsession . . . I'm using your word, Doctor, but I must put on record that I myself prefer to call it a delusion. Apart from this obsession, how did her mental state strike you?"

"She seemed to me a very normal person, a little unconventional perhaps." For a moment his eyes strayed towards the figure in the dock, still apparently impervious to all that was going on around her.

"But not likely to murder her husband for no reason?" O'Brien insisted.

"She had, or thought she had, a reason."

"Or thought she had, exactly," said O'Brien, triumphantly, and sat down again with a swirl of his gown.

Antony was back on his feet in a moment. "You wish to re-examine, Mr Maitland?" Mr Justice Carruthers asked him.

"If your lordship pleases."

Carruthers contented himself with waving a hand invitingly. "When you said she thought she had a reason, Doctor, did you not mean that no motive can be regarded as sufficient for murder?"

"Yes, Mr Maitland, that's exactly what I meant," said Macintyre, a little bewildered by this sudden substitution of one question for another. "It's very difficult," he added testily, "to say exactly what one means, when every word is taken and weighed in the balance."

"I quite agree, Doctor, it's very difficult indeed," said Antony meaningfully. "If Mr O'Brien has no further questions," – Kevin shook his head – "I think we may thank you and let you go."

There followed in the witness-box another psychiatrist of equal eminence. He was a stout man, and inclined to be more sympathetic towards Louise Chorley's predicament than Macintyre had been, but his findings had been precisely the same. Again Halloran left the examination-in-chief to his younger colleague, and again the only question that interested Antony was left unanswered: Louise Chorley had been quite adamant in not giving any clue to her lover's identity. O'Brien cross-examined on much the same lines, though, lacking the favourable climax which Dr Macintyre's answer had given him for ending his questions, he carried them a little further, trying to goad the doctor into an admission that the act in question – the murder of David Chorley – might have been committed under an insane delusion that the prisoner was thereby benefiting an imaginary lover. To this the doctor would by no means agree, and there was no need for re-examination on the prosecution's part when O'Brien gave up.

120

"But he scored a point with Dr Macintyre," said Maitland to his leader as they left the court. "She had, or thought she had, a reason," he added bitterly.

"Oh, I thought you retrieved the situation well enough," said Halloran benignly.

"Praise from Sir Hubert – " Maitland muttered. And then, "You're giving me more work with the witnesses than I bargained for."

"Sheer laziness on my part," said Halloran comfortably, though Antony knew him well enough to realise that this was manifestly untrue. "To tell you the truth I'm enjoying taking it easy," he insisted. "But the point is . . . you want the chance of cross-examining some of the defence witnesses, don't you?"

"I was hoping for one."

"Yes, exactly. Don't you think it would look a little odd if that was all the opportunity I allowed you?"

Maitland had to agree to that. "Uncle Nick must have been remarkably frank with you," he said, and wasn't quite sure whether the realisation pleased or irritated him.

"Yes, he was."

"So all that talk about not knowing what I was up to was so much hogwash. You might have told me," said Maitland.

"I might," said Halloran, and changed the subject abruptly. "Your uncle, and the rest of your family, I suppose, are worried about you. Do you realise that?"

"Of course I realise it!" Antony was annoyed now and showed it. "But Uncle Nick would do exactly the same thing in similar circumstances, and he knows it. So would Vera for that matter. And Jenny has never in her life tried to stop me from doing anything I felt was my duty. Or only once," he added, with belated honesty.

"Your uncle might desire the same ends as you do, if you're talking about finding who murdered Alan Kirby," said Halloran, "but the means he took to achieve them would be very different, I assure you."

Antony laughed aloud at that. "Yes, I suppose they would," he admitted. "And you know, Halloran, there's just about one chance in a thousand – one in a million

121

perhaps – of my being able to get anything out of any of these people in court, even under cross-examination. How far will Carruthers let me go, do you think?"

"He said once, if Mr Maitland is on one of his fact-finding expeditions, the only thing to do is to give him his head," said Halloran. "So you may be lucky."

"Yes, but this case is different. Then he could see there was a matter of justice involved, for the defendant I mean. What I want to find out won't really affect the case against Louise Chorley one way or the other."

"I think it might. It might prove that O'Brien is wrong when he says she may be mad," said Halloran flatly. "And if you can do that, my lad, I shall be eternally grateful to you."

"Oh well . . . who lives may learn," muttered Antony, a little taken aback.

They parted soon after that. Maitland thought of going back to chambers but decided against it, and let Willett – always eager to oblige – go back to the Inner Temple with his books and papers. If he had hoped to avoid his uncle by so doing, however, he was out of luck. When he let himself into the hall in Kempenfeldt Square the study door was open invitingly, and it didn't need Gibbs, hovering as usual, to tell him that Sir Nicholas would like to see him.

"You're home early, Uncle Nick," he said, as soon as he had greeted Vera suitably.

"I might say the same thing of you, my dear boy," said Sir Nicholas, who was stretched out at his ease in his favourite chair. Vera, opposite him, was knitting–a habit of hers that had made Antony nervous when first she joined the household; he wasn't sure how his uncle would put up with the click of the needles. But Sir Nicholas seemed to have borne up very well. Unfairly, as Jenny said, because he wouldn't stand it from her. The same thing might have been said of the use of slang. Vera could say exactly what she liked, and generally did, but Antony – if there weren't to be ructions – must watch his tongue.

"Carruthers adjourned early. We had the doctors this afternoon, and I think he'd had all of them he could stomach. I know I had."

122

"Even so, you may as well tell us how things went," Sir Nicholas suggested. "Jenny won't expect you for half-an-hour yet."

"All right." Antony sat down. It was colder that evening, and he was aware suddenly that he was very tired, and it would have been nice to sit there quietly watching the fire, and saying nothing at all. But his uncle must be answered, and it wasn't really a long story. "O'Brien scored a point with Macintyre," he concluded. "Halloran said it didn't matter, but I'm not so sure."

"It's never any use expecting too much of your expert witnesses, Antony."

"Don't I know it. And their chaps will be just as confident that she's as mad as a coot. I don't know who the jury will believe."

"The jury will reach its own conclusions, for no reason that any logical person can understand," said Sir Nicholas bitterly. "Now you say that with the second doctor – what was his name? – O'Brien raised the question of an act committed under an insane delusion."

"Yes, he's obviously playing on two fronts, hedging his options, whatever you like to call it."

"I should prefer you to explain exactly what you mean," said Sir Nicholas, immediately infuriated by this vagueness.

"You've already taken the point, Uncle Nick, and so has Vera. He'd like to see a verdict of Not Guilty by reason of insanity, and his client comfortably lodged in Broadmoor, but failing that he'll go for reduced responsibility. That's what the question you mentioned meant, don't you think?"

"Yes, I do."

"Like a drink before you go upstairs?" asked Vera.

"I should, very much," said Antony smiling at her, "but I think I'll wait and have one with Jenny. We shall be seeing you for dinner tomorrow evening, so we can have a longer talk then," he promised rashly. But did not realise until much later how inaccurate the prediction had been.

123

THE CASE FOR THE DEFENCE

Tuesday, the second day of the trial

The following morning was completely taken up by Kevin O'Brien's opening remarks. In essence, what he had to say was simple enough: "I'm not disputing that my client shot her husband, only that the motive was different from the one she gave the police. Can you imagine this gentle lady's shock and horror when she discovered what had been going on, as Chief Inspector Sykes admits she did when he was questioning her husband? When the shot was fired she must have been completely deranged. And later her distracted mind, seeking some comfort, hit upon this purely imaginary story of a great love. Again I must ask you to use your imagination, members of the jury, and think how this would have appealed to a woman of her nature. A poetess, whose poems are acknowledged to be sentimental, for her it must have seemed a refuge from the terrible realities of life with which she had suddenly come face to face."

That was his argument, but he elaborated on it considerably, and quoted at length from Louise Chorley's story as it had been given to *The Courier* – in essence the same as her confession to the police, but a good deal less coherent. Antony dutifully took notes of the salient points, but that was soon done. He was as glad as the judge seemed to be when Counsel for the Defence finished his speech, and gladder still when Carruthers promptly adjourned for the mid-day recess. It was, he saw with surprise, already five to twelve.

Maitland's favourite haunt at lunch-time was Astroff's Restaurant. So long as he was in London it was readily accessible wherever his professional duties might take him, and when necessary he could rely on quick service. On the other hand, if there were things to talk over and he wanted to sit half the afternoon over the meal with a companion, no waiter would hover, there would be no indication at all that they were really very much in the way. A good many lawyers from both sides of the profession patronised the restaurant for the same reason, and as that day the two counsel for the defence and the two for the prosecution had agreed to eat together, he had no difficulty in persuading them where to go.

There was a table regularly kept, until about one o'clock, at which time it was assumed that no member of Sir Nicholas's chambers would want to use it, and some less regular, less favoured customer was allowed to sit there. Antony half expected that they might encounter his uncle, but Sir Nicholas had obviously gone elsewhere. So they settled themselves at the usual table, in the corner by the window, and Halloran, always well informed in professional gossip, started on a series of anecdotes. Antony was a little surprised that their usual man didn't wait on them, and asked, as his drink was set before him, "Where's Bill today?"

"Out sick, sir. I'm taking his place, I hope you'll have no cause for complaint."

"I'm sure we shan't. You're new here, aren't you? I don't think I've seen you before."

"Started this morning, sir. Would you like to order now?"

As they had adjourned so early they were in no hurry, and decided to sit over their drinks for a while before deciding what to eat. Halloran's stories were causing some merriment, but Antony was content to sit quietly, hearing what was said but not really taking it in, his attention completely concentrated on possible forms of attack when Kevin O'Brien called his witnesses that afternoon. After a while it seemed advisable to place their order, and Halloran looked round for the waiter. As he did so, Antony pushed his chair back and got to his feet. "Move up a little, Derek," he suggested. "Uncle Nick's arrived."

Derek Stringer started to comply obligingly, and then stopped with an odd look at his neighbour. "What do you mean, Antony?" he asked. "Sir Nicholas isn't here."

"By the door," said Antony. And then turned, frowning. "I don't see him now," he said, "he must have gone out again."

"Perhaps the sight of us frightened him away," said Halloran jovially. "Where's that waiter? Ah, here you are."

"Bill!" said Antony. "I thought you were off sick."

"No, Mr Maitland."

"But you weren't here when we arrived."

"I was washing my hands," said Bill delicately. "And when I saw you gentlemen already had your drinks, and it being so early, I guessed you'd want to sit a little before you gave your order. Was that right?" he added anxiously.

"Yes, quite right. But the chap that substituted for you said he started here today."

"That's funny, I don't know of anybody new." He looked from one to the other of the men round the table. "Are you ready – ?" he began, and let the sentence trail into silence when he saw that each one of them had his attention focused on Maitland. Antony who had been still on his feet sat down again very slowly, and still more slowly began to slide down in his chair. Kevin O'Brien and Derek Stringer, on either side of him, caught his arms before he could disappear altogether under the table. "For heaven's sake!" said Halloran angrily. And then, as though it were an accusation, "You're ill!"

"Tired," said Antony. "Don't understand –"

The words trailed off, but they had been almost inaudible in any case. "I'll call a doctor," said Kevin O'Brien, perhaps the quickest witted of the three, and disappeared as Antony's eyes closed heavily, and his head fell sideways to rest on his shoulder.

He came to his senses, in surroundings that were strange to him, at about eleven o'clock that night. Not that he knew or cared about the time just then, all that mattered was that Jenny was beside him. "Where – ?" he started and broke off, seeing her anxious look. "All right, love," he said, "I'm all right. Just as weak as a kitten, that's all."

"And I don't wonder," said Jenny. "The things they've been doing to you! But Antony, I thought you might never wake up again." She'd been crying, he could see that now,

126

and though all her tears had been shed by this time, her eyes were still swollen and her voice thickened.

"No serenity," said Antony, reaching out to take her hand. "Never lose your serene look, Jenny."

"How can I look serene when you might be dying?" said Jenny, almost crossly. She allowed him to find her hand however, and was surprised and comforted by the strength of his grasp. "Uncle Nick and Vera are outside," she volunteered.

"Yes, I expect they are. The question is, where are we all?"

"You're in hospital, of course. Don't you remember anything about what happened?"

Antony frowned. "We were having lunch," he said. "Halloran, and Kevin, and Derek. And I thought Uncle Nick was going to join us, and then he went away again."

"Mr Halloran told us about that. Uncle Nick says he was never anywhere near Astroff's Restaurant today."

"Oh, I see. Well, I do remember too that it was the wrong waiter, but that's all."

"Just go to sleep now and forget about it," Jenny advised.

"Sleep? I've been asleep all day," he grumbled. "I want to know what happened. Was it food poisoning? I don't remember having lunch, and anyway I can't imagine anything like that happening there. We've eaten at Astroff's for years."

"No, it wasn't food poisoning. Do go to sleep," Jenny begged.

He began to pull himself up in the bed. "If you'll just rearrange these pillows for me, love, I could sit up quite well," he assured her. "And don't you think you ought to tell Vera I'm all right now?"

"All right!" said Jenny tragically.

"Yes, really, love. Vera will be interested to know it, even if Uncle Nick isn't."

"Antony, you know perfectly well – " Jenny began, rising to the bait as he had known she would. "Oh, all right, but I really think I ought to call the nurse first."

"I'm sure she'd have the same preoccupation with sleep

127

that you have," said Antony rebelliously. "Get Uncle Nick and Vera to come in, there's a love."

"If the nurse on duty sees me she'll know you're awake," said Jenny, but she went to the door obediently. As it happened the nurse was absent from her desk, so she beckoned in silence, and Sir Nicholas and Vera, who weren't very far away, came into the room and closed the door.

Their first enquiries, of course, were for Antony's health, and he treated them rather impatiently. A bit of a headache was all he would admit to, not even the weakness he had mentioned to Jenny, though that was by far the worst of the two problems. Also, when Kevin had grabbed his right arm, at first to prevent him from slipping further, and then to haul him back into the chair again, he had unwittingly strained Antony's shoulder badly. But that had been a forbidden subject for many years, and he saw no reason to bring it up now. "All Jenny's told me is that it wasn't food poisoning," he said. "What happened, Uncle Nick?"

"It's a bad business, Antony. What did you drink before lunch?"

"If you think I passed out on a single scotch and a lot of water, and stayed unconscious all this time," said Antony rather indignantly, "all I can say is you've a poor opinion of my capacity."

"That wasn't what I meant at all. Scotch and water, eh? The doctors tell me you were apparently given one of the quicker acting barbiturates," said Sir Nicholas precisely, "which have the added attribute of being fairly soluble and also, unless a lethal dose is given, of causing a less prolonged coma."

"Good God," said Antony, a little taken aback by all this detail. He had been puzzled before, but now was doubly so.

"That comment, I think, is more appropriate than you know," said Sir Nicholas. "I understand you might well have died—"

"I told you so!" said Jenny.

" – but they believe you must have an unusual resistance to the drug. Fortunately O'Brien and the others acted

128

quickly when you collapsed, and your own constitution did the rest." He paused, eyeing his nephew keenly, and then turned to Jenny and from her to Vera. "I really think you can stop worrying about him now, my dears," he said. "It's just a matter of time now, and rest."

"And sleep," said Antony, sourly. "Look here, Uncle Nick, I want to know the whole tale. There was a strange waiter on –"

"Precisely. After it was realised what had happened the police made extensive enquiries. The man who served you was unknown to any of the others, several of the waiters had seen him and thought that, as he told you, he was a new employee. Even the barman, who knows you well, thought the same thing and that he had just made a mistake when he ordered a double scotch for you."

"It isn't altogether unknown –"

"No, but he maintains he can tell by the way you look which it will be."

"Am I so transparent?" asked Maitland, not altogether pleased with the idea.

"He knows you well," Sir Nicholas repeated. "Besides, he could tell from the company you were keeping that you were probably in court. So he said nothing and gave you a single, which was just as well, because I don't imagine alcohol and the drug mix very well."

"I must remember to thank him. But this other waiter –?"

"He must have been watching his chance, and was lucky that Bill disappeared exactly when he did. It took some nerve, but we've all heard of cases where people have done the most extraordinary things undetected, just by looking completely at home with what they were doing, and not doing anything to attract special attention to themselves."

"But I didn't know the man."

"I don't suppose you did. Even you, I imagine, Antony, might have thought twice about accepting a drink from the hands of someone you recognised as a member of the criminal fraternity."

"I certainly should. But somebody knew" – he was speaking slowly, thinking it out – "that we usually lunch

129

there, that we usually sit at the same table, and I don't suppose for a moment that the pseudo-waiter had that information."

"No, I don't suppose so either, somebody put him up to it. The question is... who?"

For the moment Antony ignored that. "I remember I thought I saw you in the restaurant just before I collapsed," he said. "Was that part of the effect of the drug?"

"Yes, the doctors tell me hallucinations might have resulted, or a state of extreme excitement or euphoria."

"I wish somebody would induce a state of euphoria now," said Antony bitterly.

"Yes, I dare say you do. But you didn't answer my question."

"Who put the false waiter on to drugging me? Who do you think, Uncle Nick? The same person that killed Alan Kirby."

"Guesswork," said Sir Nicholas succinctly.

"Not a bit of it, a reasonable deduction," said Antony. "Isn't it, Vera?"

"Seems likely in the circumstances," said Vera gruffly. "Got to take care."

"If anybody else uses the word sleep to me, I – I don't know what I'll do. I never felt more wide awake in my life. Anyway, at Astroff's of all places. Who would have thought I could be in any danger there?"

"Astroff does his marketing on Tuesdays," said Sir Nicholas. "I wonder if our friend knew that too."

"I dare say he did, it wouldn't be difficult to find out. Poor chap – Astroff I mean – I bet he's fit to be tied."

Sir Nicholas closed his eyes. "I should prefer you to express it differently, but there can be no doubt that he's upset," he admitted. "However, my dear boy, I think it's time we left you. Jenny needs her rest if you don't."

"Just a minute, what happened in court today? Did Halloran tell you?"

"The defence's psychiatrists were called."

"Not Louise Chorley? It's customary –"

"Yes, Antony, I know quite well what's customary. But for some reason Kevin O'Brien seems to have decided to call her evidence last; perhaps he feels she will be his strongest witness. The evidence of the good doctors, I may tell you, was merely what you got from Dr Macintyre and his colleague, only reversed of course. By the time it was over news of your – shall we say accident? – had been received, and Carruthers felt it expedient to adjourn until tomorrow morning, for further news of its cause. Where you are concerned, Antony, one always expects the unusual."

"Well, God bless him for that," said Antony, ignoring his uncle's rather barbed comment. "So all the people I'm interested in –"

"Will be on the stand tomorrow, I expect, or some of them at least. Jenny, my dear –"

"Yes, you shall all have your sleep," said Antony firmly, throwing back the bed-clothes. "Wait for me in the car, it will only take me two minutes to dress."

"You're not going anywhere tonight," said his uncle flatly.

"Oh yes, I am. If I stay here until tomorrow morning I shall be too weak to move, and I must be in court."

"There's no must about it. You've done enough."

"Agree with Nicholas," said Vera.

But Jenny, who had been looking at her husband in silence, turned to them suddenly. Antony wondered later whether she realised how much her own distress at what had happened, what he had called her loss of serenity, had stiffened his resolution to find Alan Kirby's killer. "I really think he's right," she said. "Why don't you do what he suggested and wait outside, and if you see the nurse, Uncle Nick, you can tell her what Antony has decided."

They went then, though Sir Nicholas was still grumbling. Jenny found Antony's clothes and brought them to him, and helped him to put them on. She was perfectly well aware of his weakness, but even more conscious that to frustrate him in his desire to go home would do more harm than good. They didn't leave the hospital without some expostulation from the duty nurse, who threatened to call sister. But Sir Nicholas, putting on his loftiest tone, assured her that he would take all responsibility, and at last they got away.

When Maitland followed Halloran into the courtroom the next morning, the first person he saw – perhaps this was because he was looking for him – was Detective Chief Inspector Sykes, sitting on one of the benches reserved for those of the witnesses who had already given evidence, and looking as placid as usual, as though he were quite happy to wait all day for the proceedings to begin. "I'll be with you in a moment," said Antony to his leader, and made his way to the detective's side.

"I hope you're feeling better this morning, Mr Maitland," said Sykes, getting to his feet.

"And I hope you're not going to say I told you so," said Maitland, and took a quick look round to see whether there was any chance of their being overheard. But it was early yet, the public gallery looked to be full, but in the body of the court not too many people had yet taken their places.

"I told you so? Now why should I say that to you?" Sykes asked him.

"I think you know very well, Chief Inspector. You warned me of what might happen if I continued what my uncle is pleased to call my meddling."

"If you think back, you may recall that I said, If you were right in your surmise," Sykes reminded him.

"Well, doesn't this convince you that I was?" retorted Maitland, rather belligerently. "Somebody was out to – to incapacitate me at least, someone who didn't care whether I died or not."

"I see you're pretty well recovered," said Sykes smiling. "You should be thanking heaven, I suppose, for the fact that you are by nature abstemious."

"When occasion demands, I am," Antony conceded. "However, Chief Inspector–"

"I didn't expect to see you here this morning," Sykes told him, ignoring the rather portentous tone of those last words.

132

"I shouldn't be if the doctors had their way. Or my loving family either," he added and smiled. "But there's a favour I want to ask you."

This time it was Sykes who glanced round. "For once you needn't be afraid of any impropriety in your being seen talking to me," Antony reassured him. "I'm appearing for the prosecution ... remember?"

"I remember very well," said Sykes. "Is this something to do with the case?"

"Nothing whatever. I want to know if a certain gentleman of our acquaintance rents any other accommodation than the house he shares with his wife."

"Wouldn't the telephone book tell you that?"

"I don't think he'd be using his own name. It might mean a tailing job, and that's something you can manage better than I can."

"And I say to one 'Come' and he cometh, and I say to another 'Go' and he goeth," said Sykes. "Is that how you think it is, Mr Maitland?"

"I'm quite sure it is."

"Couldn't Mr Horton –"

"Of course he could, though we've no client now, remember. The trouble is, the chaps he uses are excellent but terribly slow. This is something I want doing in a hurry, tonight if possible."

"I see." The detective's look was suddenly intent. "You're absolutely serious about this, aren't you, Mr Maitland?"

"I was never more serious in my life," Antony assured him.

"One of the three men who have been called as character witnesses for Louise Chorley?" asked Sykes.

"One of them."

"Then you've eliminated young Bernard Ramsey altogether?"

"I eliminated him long since. His killing Alan didn't make sense, even if they had once quarrelled over the girl. Besides, I don't believe for a moment that he has the brains to be the organiser, and I don't think Louise is the type to appeal to him."

"No, I see. But you do realise – don't you? – that even if

133

such a hideout exists it's extremely unlikely your suspect will visit it tonight."

"Naturally I do," said Antony a little impatiently. "But there is one thing. You told me a sad little story of Nobby Clark."

"What has that to do—?"

"Wait a bit! Not that I believe for a moment," he added inconsequently, "that he broke down and confessed his sins because of the strain of living with a modern painting. But you did say he mentioned that David Chorley was his contact, and it occurred to me to wonder whether by any chance another name had come up in the same connection."

"There was another name he knew," the detective said slowly. "Just the surname—a common one—and no initial. I don't think Clark knew how to get in touch with him, even if he hadn't been in considerable awe of him. Our chaps tried, of course, but it never led anywhere."

"Then will you try it my way?"

Sykes glanced round again. The room was beginning to fill up now. "I think perhaps you'd better write the name down for me, Mr Maitland," he said cautiously.

"Then you'll do it?" said Antony, feeling in his pocket for one of his inevitable envelopes.

"Wait a bit," Sykes advised him. "Give me the name now, and then I'll think about it." And with this Maitland, for all his impatience, had to be content.

So he wrote down the name in his best printing, which at least was legible, though hardly elegant, and made his way back across the room to Halloran's side. "Have you any idea why O'Brien has altered the order of his witnesses?" he enquired.

"Not to oblige you, I imagine," said Halloran, a trifle grumpily, and gave his companion a keen look. "I know you've assured me you're all right now, Maitland, which may or may not be true. But are you sure you're fit enough to go through with this? I don't want you collapsing in the middle of cross-examination."

"I won't," said Antony, and wondered as he spoke whether he were really telling the truth. His head had stopped aching, that was one thing to be said in his favour, but his legs felt shaky and his shoulder was giving him a minor form of hell.

Carruthers entered then, before they could have any further conversation, and the prisoner was brought up from the cells below. There was a polite enquiry from the bench. "I trust you've recovered from your indisposition, Mr Maitland." And then the first witness was called.

This was Daniel Kirby. He strode into the court as if he owned it, took the oath in a very self-possessed way, and then bowed to the judge and to Kevin O'Brien who was waiting to begin his examination-in-chief.

O'Brien began on a low key with some routine questions that established the witness's identity and standing. Finally he asked, "I believe you are acquainted with my client, Mrs Louise Chorley?"

"Yes, indeed I am."

"I'm sorry, Mr Kirby, to have had to call you to give evidence in this unfortunate affair. I can only assure you that it is very far from a waste of time, but of the utmost importance to Mrs Chorley."

"No need to apologise," said Kirby in his forthright way. "I consider it an honour to be asked to speak on her behalf."

O'Brien couldn't resist a quick look at his opponent before he went on. Halloran was doodling on the back of his brief, and pretending to take no notice of the proceedings, though all his colleagues knew perfectly well that he would be on his feet in a moment at the slightest hint of irregularity. Kevin's eyes lingered on Maitland's face for a moment, and then he turned back to his witness again.

"I'm glad you feel like that, Mr Kirby," he said. "How long have you known Mrs Chorley?"

"She was a friend of my wife before we were married, they were at school together. So I've known her as long as I've been married, and that's twenty-five years next month."

"Enough time to form a pretty good estimate of her character, wouldn't you say?"

"I should indeed, though I should explain that she was more my wife's friend than mine. By that I mean that my wife had more time to spend with her, not that there were any ill relations between us."

"No, I think we all understand that perfectly. And her late husband, Mr David Chorley?"

"I believe they had been married about fifteen years, so my acquaintance with him dates from that time. But acquaintance is the word, I didn't know him nearly so well as I knew his wife. That was particularly so in later years, since I retired myself and was often there during the day when she came to tea with Mrs Kirby."

"Can you tell us, I wonder, anything about the relationship between those two people, David Chorley and his wife Louise?"

"I can't understand how she could have stood living with him for a moment," said Daniel, suddenly sounding extremely irascible, and obviously forgetting the courtroom etiquette he had schooled himself in before going into the box. "Nobody uses the word nowadays, but it's the only one to describe him . . . a bounder. They had nothing in common at all."

Kevin, not unnaturally, looked a little taken aback at this outburst. Maitland was wondering how he came to have laid himself open in this way. Neither of the defence lawyers might have seen the witness themselves, but it was no more like Derek than it was like Kevin to have made such a mistake. The trouble was, it wasn't like Mr Bellerby either, their instructing solicitor. The only conclusion was that Kirby had been considerably more careful when his proof was prepared than he was now being in court. It didn't seem to make sense, unless . . .

"You're expressing your own feelings about Mr Chorley, of course," O'Brien was saying smoothly. "If they were married for fifteen years, I hardly think his wife could have felt that way."

"No, of course she didn't. Foolish of me to say so. Whenever I saw them together they seemed to be on the best of terms."

"Can you give me some estimate of her character?"

"She wrote poetry you know," said Daniel Kirby doubtfully. "I have to admit that puts her a little outside my league."

"What sort of poetry?" asked O'Brien, who of course knew perfectly well.

"Sentimental twaddle," snapped Daniel, forgetting himself again.

"The sort of thing," said O'Brien smoothly, "in which a lady of sensibility might indulge, without in any way reflecting on her respectability?"

"Oh, certainly, certainly. A very respectable lady. And never wrote a word," said Kirby, with the first sign of humour that Antony had ever seen in him, "that might have brought a blush to a maiden's cheek."

"Thank you, Mr Kirby," said Kevin. "You have used the word 'lady', and I take it you do so advisedly."

"She's a friend of my wife," said Daniel simply.

"Quite so. A respectable lady, of a rather sentimental nature. Would it be likely do you think, Mr Kirby, that such a person would be living a double life?"

"I don't understand you, I'm afraid."

"It's quite simple. You were not in court, of course, when Mrs Chorley's confession was read. Do you think it likely that this lady whom you have described would have been deceiving her husband by having a lover?"

"Never heard of such a thing in my life."

"I take it, Mr O'Brien, that the witness means No," put in Carruthers from the bench.

"I believe he does, my lord. I am right, Mr Kirby, am I not, in thinking that you feel such a state of affairs would have been so unlikely as to be impossible?"

"Quite right."

"Would you say she had a motive for shooting her husband?" (Maitland stirred at the words, but Halloran's hand on his arm restrained him.)

"No rational motive, no."

"With his lordship's permission," said O'Brien, "I'm going to put to you a theory, put forward by one of the expert witnesses, a psychiatrist, whom the court heard yesterday. May I proceed, your lordship?"

"You may, Mr O'Brien."

"On the morning of David Chorley's death Mrs Chorley had been present when the police interviewed him, and learned for the first time (a) that he had murdered her

137

friend, Emily Walpole, and (b) that he had been part of a ring of art thieves who have been operating in this country in recent years. The witness I have mentioned feels that it is very likely that when she shot her husband she was acting out of shock and horror at finding out what had been going on, and that the story she told the police later was her imagination working to cover an intolerable fact."

"You forget, Mr O'Brien, I'm not familiar with the story Mrs Chorley told the police, only with the fact of her arrest for murder."

"I apologise." Again there was that glance at Maitland, and Antony thought suddenly, he knows perfectly well what I'm up to and he's trying to help me. But that wouldn't prevent O'Brien from doing his damnedest for his own client. "Mrs Chorley told the police that she shot her husband to protect her lover, who was the organiser of this ring of thieves. She was sure David Chorley was about to make a full confession, and he was the only person beside herself who knew this man's identity."

"Funny business," said Kirby briefly. "And you think she imagined the whole thing?"

"That is our case, Mr Kirby."

"Could be, could be."

"In other words," said O'Brien, "do you think that, in full possession of her faculties, this lady could have taken a gun and shot her husband?"

"No, I don't," said Kirby bluntly. "Not at all the sort of thing she'd do for any reason." But he was a prickly witness, and by the time O'Brien had finished the reiteration which every lawyer seems to feel is necessary if the simplest fact is to be conveyed clearly to the dimmest jury, his temper had become very short indeed.

"Feel all right?" Halloran queried. And Maitland nodded at him shortly.

"I have just a few questions for you, Mr Kirby," he said, getting to his feet. "I shan't detain you long."

"Oh, it's you, is it?" said Kirby. And then, as a sort of aside, but the words were very clearly audible, "One never knows where you fellows will turn up next."

Maitland glanced up at Mr Justice Carruthers, but met

a bland look in which he read no reason to delay his questions. "You used a very descriptive word about David Chorley, Mr Kirby," he said, turning back to the witness. "You said he was a bounder. Don't you think a sensitive lady such as you have described would have found this trying over a period of fifteen years?"

"She's a respectable woman," said Daniel Kirby, rather as if the word was a talisman.

"Respectable...ah, yes. But even a respectable woman might have a rational reason for murdering her husband, if they were on bad terms, for instance."

"I don't see why she should have killed him, she could have left him, couldn't she?"

"Now that brings us back to the other point in her statement. She shot her husband to protect her lover, and her lover was a man who had consistently been engaged in criminal activities for a number of years. It was at her instigation, she said, that David Chorley had been employed by this other man to carry out certain thefts, and if he had proved useful in this way–"

"I still say she could have left him," Kirby interrupted.

"And what – assuming her story to be true – would have been the result of that? If he resented her action, perhaps the very thing she was trying to avoid when she shot him."

"Mr Maitland," said the judge, almost apologetically.

"My lord?"

"You seem to be making a great many assumptions."

"I submit, my lord, no more than my learned friend, Mr O'Brien, was making a few moments ago."

"Very well, you may continue. But there are limits, as you know, Mr Maitland, to what I shall allow."

"If your lordship pleases." He turned back to Daniel Kirby again. "You are a collector yourself, Mr Kirby, I understand."

"Of paintings, yes. I believe my collection is considered to be a good one."

"Have you heard talk of this ring of thieves who have been operating?"

"Nobody with any interest in the trade could have

139

avoided doing so. It's talked of in the sale rooms, it's talked of in the galleries; oh yes, I've certainly heard about it."

"Your nephew, Alan Kirby—"

"What about him?"

"A painting—I believe by Rubens—was found concealed in his wardrobe in the room in the house where he lodged. He would have stood trial for receiving stolen goods, had he not been shot down in the street before the case could come on."

"Of course I know all that," said the witness impatiently. "His later period," he added. "The Rubens, I mean."

"My point, Mr Kirby—"

"Mr Maitland!" This time Carruthers coughed, perhaps to emphasise his point. "You remember my warning?"

"Indeed I do, my lord."

"I cannot feel that this matter—and I see that your friend Mr O'Brien agrees with me—is in any way relevant to the matter in hand." O'Brien was on his feet, and had been trying to catch the judge's eye.

"May I have your lordship's permission to explain?" asked Maitland. "My learned friend for the defence is concerned to show that Louise Chorley's lover did not exist, and that if he is merely a figment of her imagination, she cannot be held to be altogether in her right mind. The prosecution contends that the accused was quite sane, and that her story to the police, and subsequently to *The Courier* newspaper, was true in every respect. What better way can we find of demonstrating this than by proving the existence of the man she referred to as her lover?"

"That sounds very specious, Mr Maitland. What do you think, Mr O'Brien?"

"I agree with your lordship," said Kevin promptly. "A specious explanation for the introduction of irrelevant matter."

"All the same, Mr O'Brien, I think I shall overrule you," said Carruthers, as though an objection had actually been made. "I have found in the past that there are occasions when it pays to allow Mr Maitland to persevere. Who knows what paths he may choose to lead us down today?"

140

It was a sign of the friendship that had sprung up between O'Brien and Maitland, that Kevin didn't take this amiss but sat down and exchanged a grin with Derek Stringer. "Have I your lordship's permission to proceed?" asked Maitland, satisfied for the moment to have gained his point, but also aware that things might change at any time.

"Yes, Mr Maitland. Bearing my remarks in mind, of course."

"Of course, my lord. I was about to ask you, Mr Kirby, whether you felt that the theft of the Rubens could have been part of this larger organisation of robberies?"

"I don't see why not."

"In other words, you believe implicitly—"

"I know the thefts are taking place," Kirby interrupted again. "And nobody but an idiot could possibly believe that they weren't being organised by one man."

"Do you think Alan Kirby was guilty of receiving?"

"How can I know? I know he disliked his job, and would have liked to have had enough money to leave it and devote himself to research and writing, but whether he would have resorted to criminal means to gain that end I have no idea at all."

"It does seem, however, that the theft of the Rubens must have been connected in some way with this larger organisation?"

"I've already answered that, I think."

"You must forgive the repetition," said Maitland, as blandly as Sir Nicholas himself might have done. "I was leading into another question. Have you any reason to think that a woman being of a poetical nature would make her any the less passionate?"

"That's an extraordinary question."

"All the same, I should like an answer."

"Well no, of course it wouldn't. I said Louise was respectable, and I stick to it, but I never said she was a vegetable."

Maitland grinned at that, and would very much have liked to exchange a look with the judge, if he hadn't felt this might in some way endanger his lordship's leniency towards his cross-examination. "Then there's nothing inherently improbable in her having had an extramarital affaire?" he said.

"I'd have said she wouldn't, but today's morals are beyond me," said Daniel Kirby.

"Did you yourself have any connection with her, except as a family friend?"

"None at all. I can't remember offhand ever having seen her except in company with my wife."

"You will agree, I think," said Maitland, making a snipe flight back to a different subject, "that Alan Kirby's association with the Rubens, whether guilty or innocent, was probably prompted by his relationship to you and your known expertise in these matters?"

O'Brien was on his feet again. "My lord," he said, "Alan Kirby is not on trial."

"What have you to say to that, Mr Maitland?"

"One thing, my lord. If what I have said is true, then Alan Kirby's violent death is the third that can be attributed, more or less directly, to this organisation, and therefore to its leader."

"Three murders?" said the witness, wrinkling his brow. Maitland went on smoothly, as though there had been no interruption.

"Even if we except David Chorley's murder, to which the accused has admitted, that is two too many. Not bad going for a creature of Louise Chorley's imagination." He sat down suddenly as he finished speaking, leaving David Kirby with his mouth half open for further comment.

Kevin O'Brien re-examined, of course. That was only to be expected. "I think," said Halloran judiciously, listening to his opponent smoothing over the edges of his witness's admissions, "that you didn't do badly at all. Either from my point of view or your own," he added. And then, sarcastically, "Have you any objection to my cross-examining the next witness?"

"We agreed—"

"Yes, that you would take the men and I would take the women. I hope that doesn't seem too unreasonable to Carruthers. However, I believe Daniel Kirby's wife is coming on stage next...and you look as if you could do with a rest," he added with some concern.

"Yes, I think I could," Maitland admitted. "But you will remember, won't you –?"

"I'll remember anything you like," said Halloran gruffly, "provided you don't keep pushing notes under my nose as you did when I was presenting my case for the prosecution."

Antony grinned at that, and sat back in his place to listen. Daniel Kirby was a big man in all senses of the word, a virile man; just then Maitland would have given a good deal to know exactly what Louise Chorley was really like.

The next witness, as Halloran had predicted, was Mrs Hilda Kirby, and Kevin O'Brien found her much more rewarding than her husband. She had known Louise Chorley since they had both been about ten years old. "No, that's not quite correct, I was eleven and she was ten. She was clever, you know, and always in a class just above her own age group."

"But you had the opportunity of knowing her well?"

"Very well indeed. We were at boarding-school together, and of course that meant we saw a good deal of each other, both in class and out of it."

"Circumstances dictated a certain intimacy then. Did friendship lead you to seek her out even more often?"

"Yes, it did. Now I wonder if I am giving you exactly the right impression. I said she was clever, and of course I admired her tremendously. I've sometimes wondered whether I sought her out, as you put it, more often than she liked."

"Have you any reason for thinking that?"

"No, not really. She was always very patient with me."

"I wonder why you should say that, Mrs Kirby?"

"Because I was so dull. We used to go on walks together, and she'd teach me poems I had to know for the next day, things like that. Or explain something to me that I didn't understand."

"In other words, a kind-hearted person?"

"Oh, yes, yes I'm sure that's true. There were three of us who were very close; my cousin Constance, who's Con-

143

stance Shields now, was the third. When we had to write poetry ourselves – and I don't understand why, but our elocution mistress had a craze for asking us to do that – Louise used to write one for each of us. It certainly simplified matters."

"Now I know very little of what goes on in a girls' school," said Kevin O'Brien obviously. "You've said my client was kind-hearted, and it certainly seems to have been the case where her friends were concerned. But with people outside your own little group, was she any different?"

Maitland, looking across, was pretty sure that O'Brien knew this time what to expect. "Well, of course, the question didn't arise," said Hilda. "I don't know if I'm explaining exactly what I mean, she used to help Connie and me, but no one else would have thought to ask her. She was certainly never unkind to anybody."

"And as you grew up, did you have any occasion to change this favourable opinion of her?"

"Oh no, none at all."

"She was married a little late in life, I think your husband said, about ten years after you were?"

"Eight or nine years after, I think. I could tell you the date of her wedding, but not the year. No, no, let me think. I remember that it occurred to me at the time that it was nine years after our own, only not the same month of course."

"How did you like David Chorley?"

"He was" – she hesitated – "an exuberant man. I ought to explain that–"

"I think the word is explanation enough in itself, Mrs Kirby."

"No, I don't want to mislead you. To tell you the truth, I don't think Daniel – my husband – cared for him overmuch. He was, I think you could say, bouncy. But I wouldn't want you to think he wasn't a very nice person."

"Do you think his wife thought that of him too?"

"Yes, I'm sure she did."

"They got on well together?"

Halloran was on his feet. "I think, M'lud–"

144

"Really, Mr Halloran, it is only a matter of phrasing," said Mr Justice Carruthers. He turned to the witness. "Did Mr and Mrs Chorley get on well together?" he asked.

Hilda was definitely confused at this sudden question from the bench, and hesitated a little over her reply. "Oh yes, indeed," she said. "Louise wasn't the sort of person to quarrel with anybody, and David was the soul of good humour."

"Thank you, my lord," said Kevin O'Brien a little ironically. "Now Mrs Kirby, you have described your friend to us as she was in her younger years. Do you think there was any change recently?"

"No, I never saw any difference in her. I ought to explain," she added anxiously, "we used to have a joke together that she was a business woman now, whereas I had no occupation except being a housewife. I mean, of course, her poems. You know they were all published in the newspaper, and then there were the booklets, such pretty bindings, that was Constance's husband's doing, you know. I think he thought the world of her."

"But essentially, Mrs Kirby, did she stay the same?"

"Oh yes, I think so."

"You mean by that kind-hearted, intelligent, and – may I use the term? – faithful to her husband?"

"I would certainly never have thought anything else of her."

"A sensitive woman?" Halloran rolled an eye in Antony's direction, but did not again intervene.

"Yes, indeed, very sensitive."

"Speaking frankly, had she a motive to shoot her husband?"

"I read of her arrest, that's really all I know about it, you know. It isn't the sort of thing that happens to one's friends."

"Well, leaving that aside for the moment, madam, living together in harmony as you believe them to have been, do you think she had any motive for such an act?"

"No."

"No rational motive?" O'Brien insisted.

"Yes, I think that's what I meant."

"But if she had just heard her husband being questioned

by the police, and had realised that for some time, without her knowledge, he had been engaged in criminal activities, don't you think she might have reacted in shock and horror, without really knowing what she was doing, by taking his life?"

"It could only have been that way. Of course, we read all about the inquest on David Chorley, and the things he had been doing. I hope I'm making myself clear, it would certainly have been terrible for Louise."

"A terrible shock?" O'Brien insisted again.

"Yes, yes that's what I meant."

"In other words, do you think that your friend, in her right mind, could have possibly done such a thing?"

"No, I don't."

This time O'Brien didn't attempt to get any repetition of these statements, but was content to let well alone. Halloran lumbered to his feet. "I wonder, madam, if you do not mean by that last reply that murder is not usually the resort of a rational person. Everyone, even the most sane amongst us, must be at such time a little – shall we say? – outside himself."

Again Hilda Kirby was confused by the question coming from a different quarter. "Yes, I think that's exactly what I meant," she said doubtfully.

"You may or may not know, Mrs Kirby, that during the last few years there has been a succession of thefts of valuable paintings throughout the country, which are believed to be the result of one man's organisation."

"I knew about that, of course, Daniel has often spoken of it; though he knows," she added with a little resentment in her tone, "that I'm not in the least interested in art. And, of course, there's everything that came out at David's inquest, I wouldn't have believed it of him."

"You mean, I think, that you would be unwilling to think ill of any of your friends."

"Yes, of course."

"Then your opinion of Louise Chorley may have been the result of some prejudice in her favour?"

"Do you think so? I always found her a perfect lady."

"But you yourself are a charitable woman? Charitable in your thoughts about others, I mean."

"I hope so."

"And you wouldn't think Louise Chorley would be the sort of person to engage in relations with a man not her husband?"

"No, certainly not. I'm trying my best to make myself clear, I mean I know I'm on oath. And in some ways Louise could be a little . . . Bohemian," said Hilda, unconsciously echoing the judge's thought. "But not to that extent."

"However, you will agree I'm sure, Mrs Kirby, that two people of completely dissimilar temperament, living together for fifteen years, might at the end of that time have found themselves on bad terms. In other words, that some rational motive might have existed for Louise Chorley killing her husband."

"I don't think Louise was ever very rational," said Hilda Kirby, confounding him.

"Nevertheless," said Halloran, "I'm sure you will agree that a sensitive, poetical nature does not imply that the owner of these attributes would be any less passionate because of them?"

"Passionate?" She sounded as though somehow the word itself made her afraid. "I agree with . . . with the gentleman I was talking to before. I don't think Louise would have had a lover."

"It was you who used the word Bohemian, Mrs Kirby," Halloran reminded her.

"Yes, indeed I did. I'm explaining myself very badly. I meant it in a respectable way," said the witness, confused.

"We spoke a moment ago about the art thefts, Mrs Kirby."

"Yes, but I don't see what they have to do with this."

"We're agreed, are we not, that in view of Louise Chorley's statement to the police they must have something to do with it?"

"I don't really know anything about her statement."

"She said she had a lover who was the organiser of the thefts, and that she shot her husband to protect this other man."

"Oh dear, oh dear. She couldn't have meant it I'm sure,"

147

said Hilda, just as though this was the first mention she had heard of possible infidelity.

"What I was going to ask you, madam, was whether your nephew, Alan, could have had anything to do with these thefts?"

"Alan would never do anything wrong, anything at all."

"His death is the third, directly or indirectly, that has been caused by the thefts. Don't you think it's time they were stopped?"

"I don't know what the police are thinking about," she said severely.

Halloran smiled at that, which indeed was answer enough. "One last question, Mrs Kirby," he said encouragingly. "I understand that your friendship with Mrs Chorley became, after your marriage, very much a family affair. Can you think of anyone with whom she was on terms of intimacy, outside this normal group?"

"Nobody at all."

"For instance," said Halloran, "did your husband, to your knowledge, ever meet her outside the family home? Something as innocuous as a luncheon date, it might be."

He sat down again without waiting for the witness's reply, a bewildered, "No, never." Kevin O'Brien had not even time to voice an objection.

Neither did he choose to re-examine her, which was probably as well for all concerned. It was growing late, Mr Justice Carruthers was hungry, and adjourned for the luncheon recess without further ado.

That day the four of them went to Astroff's Restaurant again, and Bill, who seemed to think that Monday's debacle had been all his fault, made a great fuss of Maitland, going so far as to make a special arrangement with the kitchen to provide him with a rather bland bowl of soup, and some Perrier water from a bottle which he insisted on opening himself. Not that anybody was worried that the same trick would be played again, anybody except Bill, that is.

"You were lucky," said O'Brien amiably, "that we got

148

Carruthers. He's used to your tricks, Antony, but I don't think anybody else would have been so lenient."

"Tricks?" said Maitland, spooning his soup. "I wasn't aware—"

"Oh, come off it," said Derek Stringer, who was a friend and colleague of long standing, and wasn't going to put up with any nonsense of this sort. "You know perfectly well what O'Brien means."

"My learned friend," said Halloran subduing his booming voice as well as he could out of deference to the rest of the customers, "gave an explanation to the judge which his lordship decided to accept. That's all there is to it."

"Be that as it may," said O'Brien firmly, "we're going to win this case."

"That, we shall see. And meanwhile," said Halloran, "let's talk of something less controversial." Which surprised Maitland because he was pretty sure it was out of consideration for his feelings, and he was more used to expecting sarcasm than sympathy from his leader.

That day they ate in rather more of a rush, because Kevin O'Brien's re-examination of Daniel Kirby had taken some time, and Mr Justice Carruthers had a well known dislike of sitting late. They were barely back in their places before the judge appeared, and the prisoner was produced and the next witness, Raymond Shields, was called.

Antony took time for a good look at Louise Chorley. Not that he had neglected her that morning, particularly while Halloran was cross-examining Hilda Kirby, but if any crack appeared in the wall she seemed to have built up around herself he wanted to be the first to notice it. As it was, she was still sitting there blankly, having been guided again to her chair by the wardress, staring straight in front of her, apparently not recognising anybody at all. So for the time being he could turn his attention to the witness, and to the preliminary questions which O'Brien was getting through with practised speed.

Raymond Shields, as perhaps might have been expected, seemed just as self-possessed as Daniel Kirby had done, not at all as if he found his present position an uncomfortable one. Inevitably O'Brien reached the question, "How long have you known my client, Mrs Louise Chorley?"

149

"That takes a bit of thinking about," Shields admitted. "Let's see, my wife knew her all her life or thereabouts, and I must have met Louise about the same time I first met Constance. We've been married for nearly twenty years, and I knew her at least four years before she consented to be my wife."

Kevin O'Brien glanced down at the note his junior pushed before him, probably the result of this rather complicated calculation. "In that case," he said, "I take it you knew her well?"

"Yes, certainly."

"Was it because of your wife's influence that you first began to publish Mrs Chorley's poems?"

"No, not at all. My wife's line is art. In fact," said Shields, settling himself with an elbow on the ledge of the witness box, as though looking forward to a pleasant gossip, "I'd really say she had a good deal more in common with Dan Kirby than Hilda has."

"Then her taste doesn't run to literature?"

"If you can call the kind of stuff I publish literature," said Shields doubtfully.

"I'm not very familiar with it," said Kevin O'Brien tentatively, obviously fascinated with this particular publisher's own view of himself and his works.

"Cookery books... you can't call a recipe literature. And books about gardening, the same thing applies. The nearest we came, I suppose, to anything of quality were the books of local historical interest. I must say young Alan Kirby, Dan's nephew, did a pretty good job on those. Not that he cared about that, it wasn't what he wanted to be doing at all. As for Louise's poems, I'm very sure you couldn't call them literature either."

"Why did you publish them then?"

"They were popular," said Shields simply. "In fact they sold in great quantities. One of our staple lines, I don't know what I shall do without her."

"Please, Mr Shields, you mustn't prejudge the issue," said O'Brien before Carruthers could speak. "Then you had a business relationship with Mrs Chorley, quite apart from the personal one you had through her friendship with your wife?"

150

"That's quite correct. As to the personal relationship," said Shields, who seemed to have a passion almost equal to Hilda Kirby's for explaining himself, "I should say it was more our friendship with the Kirbys that led to our seeing Louise from time to time. She and Hilda were very good friends, but Constance, I think, was a little worried by the sentimental nature of the poetry she wrote. But, of course, Constance and Hilda being cousins, we had a close relationship with the Kirbys, and as I say it was through them that we saw something of Louise."

"Thank you Mr Shields," said Kevin, not sounding the least bit grateful. "Perhaps you'll be good enough to tell us then, your estimate of the character of the lady who is my client."

"Well now! She always seemed to be in deadly earnest about those poems of hers, thought they would cheer people up, things like that. In fact, almost as though it was her duty to write them. And sometimes, you know, that irritated me a bit, she was so very serious about her work. But on the personal level, I've nothing but praise for her. A good sort of woman, rather gentle. I don't think I can put it any better than that."

"Then may we turn to her husband, David Chorley?"

"If you want my opinion," said Shields confidentially, "Dan Kirby couldn't stand the sight of him."

"M'lud!" said Halloran, outraged.

"Just answer the questions, Mr Shields," said Carruthers quite kindly to the witness.

"Yes, my lord. I was only trying to explain that I didn't really know David very well. I usually saw Louise socially when he was away, and Hilda had invited her to join us for dinner, out of the goodness of her heart I suppose."

"Thank you, Mr Shields," said O'Brien again, with a wary look for the judge. "I wonder if you can tell us, however, what you considered their relationship to be?"

"Louise and David? Nothing out of the way. They weren't at each other's throats, I can tell you that, and Louise always spoke very nicely about him when I saw her at the office."

"Did he appreciate her work?" asked O'Brien. Maitland had long since realised that some of Counsel for the

Defence's questions were being asked in the spirit of pure curiosity, not because they advanced his case at all.

"Oh, I shouldn't think so," said Shields cheerfully.

"Was she sensitive on the subject?"

"Yes, I should say she was. I know I was always very careful myself in what I said to her, one can't afford to offend a small gold mine. And I expect David was equally careful. Certainly I never heard anything to suggest otherwise."

"Now what did you think, Mr Shields, when you read in the newspaper that Mrs Chorley had been arrested for the murder of her husband?"

"I thought there must have been some mistake. Then there was the inquest, and all those revelations about what Chorley had been up to."

"You think that explained matters?"

"I think the shock of what she had discovered about him must have sent her round the bend," said Shields firmly.

Mr Justice Carruthers looked up. "Round the bend, Mr O'Brien?" he asked plaintively.

"I think the witness meant that this new knowledge drove her insane, my lord. Is that so, Mr Shields?"

"Sounds a bit extreme, put that way," said Raymond Shields reflectively. "Still that's more or less what I meant."

"You can think of no rational motive for her shooting her husband?" asked O'Brien, picking up the defence's word.

"None at all."

"And do you think she was the sort of person to have deceived her husband, to have taken a lover?" asked O'Brien.

"That's not a thing you go around thinking about your friends," said Shields. "Whatever put the idea into your head?"

"Mrs Chorley's confession, which has been read to the court, stated that she had shot her husband to defend her lover."

"How would it help the man, whoever he was?"

"The defence's contention is that this man does not exist," O'Brien explained. "However, the prosecution

152

seem to be working on the theory that he was the head of an organisation of art thieves, and if you read the account of the inquest on David Chorley you will know that he was working for them."

"And Louise thinks she was this other man's mistress. That's a lot of nonsense. I know she's an attractive woman," said Raymond Shields, turning to look at the quiet figure in the dock, "if she didn't get herself up so arty crafty, but I ask you!"

"The witness has some question he wishes to put to the court?" asked Carruthers of O'Brien courteously.

"I think, my lord, it was merely an exclamation of incredulity. And I think, Mr Shields, you were telling me that you consider my client unlikely to have murdered her husband in cold blood and while in full possession of her senses."

"You chaps put things very well," said Raymond Shields amiably. "That's exactly what I'm trying to tell you."

That was too good an exit line; O'Brien sat down without further ado. Maitland, after an anxious glance at his leader in case Halloran had changed his mind again, came to his feet.

"You have implied, Mr Shields, that the accused and her husband were on reasonably good terms. That they got on as well as anybody else. Are you aware, I wonder, that in a case of murder the victim's nearest and dearest are always the first people to come under police scrutiny?"

"I'll take your word for it," Shields told him.

"Then can you be sure that some perfectly commonplace motive for this killing did not exist? One that would not call for my learned friend's rather fanciful theories?"

"People are always surprising you," said the witness. "But as for fanciful theories, I don't really follow you. He" – jerking his head towards O'Brien – "thinks she must have been mad to do it, and so do I."

If this went on there would be Halloran tugging at his gown and wanting to take his place. "The theory is that the accused committed the crime under the influence of extreme shock and horror at what her husband had been doing, and that the story about her having a lover is pure invention."

153

"It's a bit difficult to follow, but a purely spiritual person like Louise—"

"Are you so sure of that? Her relationship with her husband for instance, do you suppose that was on a purely spiritual plane?"

"I'm damned sure it wasn't—beg pardon, my lord—when they were first married. If you'd ever met David Chorley you'd know that." (Antony, who had, could well believe it.) "But I dare say things had cooled off a bit over the years."

"I see. You're obviously quite familiar with the fact that a gang of art thieves is operating in this country and has been for some years. You say you read of David Chorley's inquest—"

"Yes, but that wasn't when I first heard of it. My wife Constance has been full of the subject. I said earlier she's an expert on paintings, for all she's pretty modest about it. She and Daniel Kirby would often discuss the matter."

"I'm glad no further explanation is necessary. You also know that Alan Kirby, whom you mentioned earlier as being in your employ, was shot down in the street the other day?"

"I know that, I wish I didn't."

They were getting on to dangerous ground again, but Carruthers made no sign. "One way or another, whether he was innocent or guilty, his death seems to be tied up with this organisation," said Maitland. "If that is so, that is three deaths now which have their roots in the thefts, though David Chorley's only indirectly."

"Three deaths?" said Shields, astonished.

"I told you before, Mr Maitland, I do not consider this matter material," said Carruthers coldly. "There is also the question of the three deaths to which you keep referring."

"A slip of the tongue, my lord," said Maitland hurriedly.

"Twice on your part, and once on Mr Halloran's," said the judge pensively. "However, your statement to the witness hardly constitutes a question, so there is no need for him to answer it."

"I am obliged to your lordship," said counsel meaninglessly, and turned back to Raymond Shields again. "You have described to us how you met Mrs Chorley socially, in company with your wife and Mr and Mrs Kirby as a general rule. What about your meetings with her on a business basis. Were these conducted solely in your office?"

"No, we would meet for lunch sometimes, to discuss what she had ready for me. The main thing was to get a group of the poems together suitable for the Christmas trade, and that meant getting them out in good time as you can imagine."

"And you still maintain—?"

But what Counsel might have been about to say was interrupted without ceremony by the witness. "I still maintain she was spiritual rather than passionate by nature," said Shields firmly. "And that she could never, never in a hundred years, have shot her husband while she was in her right mind."

There was a moment's pause while Antony wondered whether there was anything to be done to retrieve the situation from Halloran's point of view. Then he decided there wasn't, and sat down again. He encountered a cold look from his leader, who was rapidly recovering from the concern he had felt that morning. But on his own account he was not ill pleased with the way things were going.

Constance Shields followed her husband into the witness box, and Maitland, watching his learned friend, Mr O'Brien, could tell that Counsel for the Defence, weighing her up at lightning speed during the preliminary questions, was hoping great things of her. A woman, and therefore more likely to be sympathetic to the prisoner; but a woman, it was to be hoped, of more strength of mind than Hilda Kirby, who had said the right things but in such a worried way that they might not have carried much weight with the jury.

O'Brien began with the customary question. "How long have you known my client, Mrs Louise Chorley?"

"We were at school together."

Kevin waited a moment for her to say something further on the subject, but she had answered the question and apparently thought this was all that was required of her,

155

as indeed in a sense it was. Counsel said tentatively, "Perhaps you can tell us a little more about those days."

She gave him a sudden, quite brilliant smile. "It's so long ago," she apologised. "I can't think why you should want to know what Louise was like then."

"Put it down to curiosity," said O'Brien, responding at once to this touch of friendliness. "But please believe me, Mrs Shields, the court will be very much obliged for any information you can give us. And it may be very important indeed for your friend."

"Well," said Constance, and shut her eyes for a moment to think about it. "Hilda – you know, my cousin, Hilda Kirby – always had a sort of hero-worship for Louise. Louise liked that, and did what she could to foster it. I think myself I'll have to admit she was a bit of a show-off." She paused and smiled again. "There, you see, you're tricking me back into the language of the school room."

"Would you agree with Mrs Kirby that she was a good-natured girl, and on good terms with everyone?" O'Brien had the grace to glance at Halloran as he spoke, but Counsel for the Prosecution made no sign.

"If you mean her attitude towards the others, yes that was very good. But she wasn't exactly popular, because she hated games. She was considered a bit of a swot, and that might not have been so bad if only she'd been willing to share her talent for turning out verse by the yard."

"But I understood from Mrs Kirby – ?"

"Oh yes, she was quite right, if she said that Louise would help *us* out any time we needed it. What I meant was, the poems were all . . . shall we say serious in nature. No lampoons on our schoolmistresses, or anything like that."

"In other words, she was a perfectly ordinary girl."

"I expect," said Constance, "you've heard the word Bohemian applied to her already. Even as a girl she was inclined that way."

"I think we're going to need an exact description of what you mean by that, Mrs Shields. To me it has always implied a certain – a certain looseness of morality."

Constance grinned again. "There'd have been no chance for anything like that at our school," she told him.

"Anyway, it wasn't what I meant. I meant in the way she dressed, she even managed to make a gym-slip look exotic somehow. And her manner. I always used to think of the song in one of the Gilbert and Sullivan operas. *If she's content with a vegetable love which would certainly not suit me* – do you know the one I mean?"

"Bunthorne," said Kevin O'Brien, obviously wanting to keep on the right side of this rather unpredictable witness; who was, however, turning out as he had first expected, ideal for his purpose. He was certainly not the man to neglect an opportunity, and diverged at once from his previous line of questioning. "Would you say she maintained this characteristic into later life?"

"Oh yes, indeed I would. I've heard my husband refer to her as spiritual, which is really his way of justifying the fact that he publishes the stuff she writes," she added confidentially. "But it's really a good enough word for her."

"Not the sort of lady, then, to indulge in an affaire outside her marriage?"

"Decidedly not. I think, if you really want my opinion, that she married David Chorley because marriage was the sort of life we were all brought up to expect. I think she found that side of the bargain rather unpleasant from the beginning."

"The sexual side?"

"That's what I meant. Not that she said anything, but after all I've known her for a long time, and known her very well."

"I think I had better acquaint you, Mrs Shields, with the contents of my client's confession. You read the account of the inquest on David Chorley, I suppose."

"Yes, of course I did. Every word I could find on the subject, in fact. I'm only human you know, and I was frantically curious."

"Surprised that Louise Chorley should have done such a thing?"

"It isn't the sort of thing one expects to read about one's friends," Constance pointed out.

"No, indeed. You will know then that David Chorley had been involved in art thefts, and that out of these had arisen a motive for him to murder a good friend of theirs, Emily Walpole. Mrs Chorley says in her confession that his involvement had been instigated by her, that the organiser of the thefts – which apparently are very widespread – had been her lover for many years, and that she was afraid her husband would give him away if he was arrested."

"I should say that's a lot of nonsense myself," said Constance Shields bluntly.

"Exactly, madam. Exactly what I think," said O'Brien cordially. And this time he glanced at the judge, but Carruthers was giving him his head. "We maintain that the first Mrs Chorley knew of her husband's crimes was when the police interviewed him on the day of his death. It is not very hard to imagine –"

"You may make a speech to the jury later, Mr Halloran," said Carruthers, who apparently had, after all, only been biding his time. "If you have any more questions for the witness we shall all be glad if you will ask them."

"If your lordship pleases. Two questions then, Mrs Shields," said Kevin, making the best of it. "Do you think the revelation of what her husband had been doing would have come as a shock to Mrs Chorley?"

"Of course it would, how could it be otherwise?"

"Enough to . . . to unhinge her, say?"

"If you mean to unhinge her mentally, yes, I think it would."

"Can you, in fact, think of any possible motive that would have induced her to shoot her husband while in full possession of her senses?"

"I have to say No. I find it impossible to visualise Louise with a gun at all."

"Thank you, madam," said O'Brien, looking rather like the cat who has just swallowed the cream. "I have no more questions."

Halloran was on his feet almost before his opponent had seated himself again. "You've implied, Mrs Shields," he said, "that the accused was ill-at-ease with her husband, on a physical plane, from the beginning of their marriage. Mentally would you say they were any more compatible?"

158

"No, I don't think I should. I tried to describe Louise—"

"I think we have got a fairly good picture of Mrs Chorley from what you have told us," Halloran conceded.

"Yes, but David Chorley was quite different. The complete extrovert," said Constance after a moment spent searching for the word. "Only, you know, we none of us saw so much of him, so I've no real reason to say they didn't get on."

"I think, Mrs Shields, that you are not without imagination. Two natures such as theirs, married I believe for fifteen years—"

Again she interrupted him eagerly. "Yes, I know, you'd think they'd have irritated one another terribly. But Louise lived in a world of her own; that could never have given her a motive to kill him."

"Let us examine the word Bohemian. You used it, you said, without the usual connotation of what I believe my learned friend called moral slackness. Do you not think that subconsciously you may have been giving it a wider meaning?"

"No, I don't."

"You wouldn't say, for instance, that being of a poetical nature – of a spiritual turn of mind if you prefer it – would necessarily make a woman any the less capable of passion?"

"No, I wouldn't say that. I only say that wasn't like Louise."

"My learned friend spoke of art thefts in which David Chorley was involved. Had you heard about them before you read the account of the inquest?"

"Oh yes, indeed I had. I think it was Mr Kirby, Mr Daniel Kirby, who first mentioned them to me. After that I seemed to hear talk about them everywhere, and of course I began to notice the bits in the paper, that hadn't meant anything to me before."

"Did you know Alan Kirby?"

"Of course I did, and the accusation against him was monstrous. I suppose you're implying that he might be one of the thieves, but I'm sure that wasn't so. I was furious

159

when I read of his death, but you can't blame Louise for that."

"That would certainly be difficult. I am only trying to establish the fact that the man whom it seems fashionable to call the organiser of these thefts does in fact exist."

"I don't think there's any doubt about that. But to connect Louise with him is quite another matter."

"Do you think her incapable of a passionate attachment of that nature?"

"I certainly do. And if you knew her you'd realise it's just the sort of story she would invent, a fairytale, the more unlikely the better, to distract her from the difficulties of real life."

"You say you saw more of Louise Chorley than you did of her husband." Halloran had been badly mauled, but he wasn't quite ready to give up yet.

"Yes, that's right. Raymond and I – that's my husband – used to dine with the Kirbys quite often; and if David was away, as sometimes happened, Louise would be included in the invitation too."

"At whose suggestion?"

"I don't think anybody's in particular. It had just become a habit, and either Hilda or I, whichever of us was giving the party, would ask her automatically."

"But in the first place," Halloran persisted, "the idea must have come from somewhere."

"If you're trying to make me say, Dan Kirby was this mythical lover of Louise's, it's quite out of the question."

"I'm not trying to make you say anything, madam. But why do you pick on Mr Kirby?"

"He's the only one I know with the requisite knowledge to have organised these art thefts you keep talking about. After all, whoever's doing it has to know his subject backwards, and also to know who's got the collecting bug badly enough to be willing to pay good money for a picture he could never display to his friends. But it's absolutely ridiculous to think–"

"The suggestion was yours, Mrs Shields, not mine. And Mr Kirby, as his lordship is about to point out to us, is not the subject of this investigation. Have you any recent knowledge of the accused's life apart from these occasional dinner parties?"

"She had other friends, of course. And she had her work, she was really serious about that."

"Do you know of anyone whom she was in the habit of entertaining at home in her husband's absence, or of meeting elsewhere, perhaps?"

"You're back on the subject of the lover again," said Constance scornfully. "I don't know about home, but she certainly had luncheon engagements, things like that. With my own husband for one, he's her publisher, and I expect she had to meet people from *The Courier* too when she was arranging for them to publish her poems. They always took them first, and then Raymond would collate them."

"Thank you, Mrs Shields, I have no further questions," said Halloran. Carruthers eyed him with a little amusement, and promptly adjourned for the day; a little early, but perhaps he was prompted by consideration for Mr Maitland, whom he thought to be looking both pale and tired. He didn't even wait to ask Kevin O'Brien if he wished to re-examine, there was obviously no reason on earth for him to do so. Everything was going his way. Nor was Maitland quite so happy with the way things were going as he had been at an earlier stage in the proceedings.

In consideration of Antony's status as a semi-invalid, Sir Nicholas and Vera waited until after dinner to come upstairs and demand an account of his day. "Halloran called before I left chambers," said Sir Nicholas. "He sounded a little testy."

"I don't wonder at that," Antony told him. "Everything went wrong today. From our point of view, I mean."

"From the point of view of the prosecution?"

"What else? I must say it isn't a role that appeals to me," he added thoughtfully. "But otherwise...oh, I don't know, Uncle Nick. Time will tell."

"If it has a chance," said Vera. "I hope you're taking care."

"I am, indeed." He grinned at her affectionately. "No

161

more meals out unless I'm quite sure who the waiter is, and no wandering about the streets either."

"And when do you think it will be over?" asked Sir Nicholas, with a glance at Jenny to see how she was taking this. Her brown curls were a little more untidy than usual, and she had lost what Antony always called her serene look, in favour of a sort of restlessness that was very uncharacteristic. But, as usual, she wasn't saying anything.

"Tomorrow should end it one way or the other," Antony told his uncle.

"Halloran says he's going to lose his case."

"Yes, but I don't care terribly about that," Antony admitted. "Not that I don't agree with him about where the accused belongs. The last witness, Mrs Constance Shields, was the victim of a fixed idea about Louise Chorley, and nothing anybody could say would have shaken her. Besides, I don't think she liked Louise very much really, and that made her evidence in her favour all the more telling."

"You'd better start at the beginning," said Sir Nicholas, rather as if he were obliging his nephew by the request, instead of following what had been his fixed intention in coming upstairs.

"There isn't really much to tell, except what Halloran seems to have said already."

"Well," said Sir Nicholas with exaggerated patience, "for one thing, what did the witnesses say when they saw you? After your interviewing them about Alan Kirby they must have been surprised to see you on the side of the prosecution in this case."

"It didn't seem to surprise them particularly. In fact, I think only Daniel Kirby recognised me. He made some comment about 'you chaps cropping up everywhere,' but I don't think he was much surprised."

"And none of the others—?"

"No, but I've been told often enough I look very different in my wig. It isn't as if I'm fair like you, Uncle Nick. I don't really think it was surprising if they didn't connect me with the man they'd seen before."

"Perhaps not. And the other thing I should like to know

is how they reacted to the sight of their friend in the dock?"

"That's difficult to say too. You see, Louise Chorley has been playing it dumb ever since the trial started. She doesn't look to right or left, and seems completely unaware of her surroundings. She moves quite docilely when the wardress guides her, either into or out of the dock, or to stand, or to sit. But for all anyone could tell she was quite unconscious of ever having seen any of these people before."

"So there was no indication in her attitude towards the two men—"

"No, but I think that would be something she'd be very careful about. I don't believe in this attitude of hers any more than Halloran does. I think it's carefully rehearsed, and that the idea occurred to her after she made her statement to the police, but before *The Courier* article."

"Well, that's one point of view, but the question I asked you was different. How did the witnesses react to her?"

"Hilda Kirby was the only one who kept looking at her. She was obviously acutely conscious of Louise's presence the whole time she was giving evidence, and afterwards when she was sitting in the body of the court. Daniel Kirby — there's a clever man, Uncle Nick — gave her one look, and then ignored the fact that she was present. It was much the same with both the Shields, Raymond and his wife, Constance. You know — it's an odd thing to say in this day and age when people are so lax in these matters — but I think each one of them was conscious of having taken an oath to tell the truth, and was doing his or her best to abide by it. Hilda Kirby was the only one who mentioned that fact, she was one of those nervous witnesses, terribly concerned to get everything exactly right. But I think that though the subject wasn't mentioned again the others were equally conscious of it. Telling the truth wasn't always a hundred percent complimentary to their friend, Mrs Chorley, so I'm not surprised they didn't keep looking in her direction."

It cannot be said that Sir Nicholas's curiosity (and, it must be admitted, anxiety) was completely satisfied by these answers, but seeing that his nephew looked tired he forbore to ask any more questions, and he and Vera left soon after. There was a phone call from Chief Inspector Sykes just before the Maitlands went to bed; he had nothing to report. "And I don't honestly see how you could have expected it, Mr Maitland," he said bluntly.

"I didn't," said Antony sadly. "I just hoped." And then, formally, "Thank you for the trouble, Chief Inspector."

"It wasn't I who was troubled," said Sykes, with his usual precision. "How are you getting on with Mr Halloran?"

"I'm used to him," said Antony, as though this was sufficient answer, which perhaps it was. "And in case you're thinking of commenting on what's been going on in court . . . tomorrow is also a good day." But it must be admitted that he didn't really think it would be.

Thursday, the fourth day of the trial

Except for the ache in his shoulder, which was perhaps a little more insistent than usual, Maitland felt fully recovered the following morning. All the same, he was troubled by some feelings of trepidation as he went into court, not because he expected a few plain words from Halloran before the proceedings started, but because – less preoccupied now with his own feelings of weakness – his anger over Alan Kirby's death was back in the forefront of his mind. That this anger was mixed with a sense of guilt didn't help matters. Any of his friends would have told him that this was irrational, but the assurance wouldn't have had the slightest effect on his mood. There was, besides, the added, more slow-burning but even deeper anger at the effect the poisoning attempt had had on Jenny, and there was some guilt mixed up in that too.

Bruce Halloran was as grumpy as he had expected, and perhaps it was just as well that they hadn't long to wait before everyone was in his allotted place, and Kevin O'Brien called his first witness of the day, Ernest Connolly. Counsel for the Defence had been expecting Constance Shields to deliver the goods as far as he was concerned, and how right he had been! This morning it was clear that he had no such hopes of Ernest Connolly, except insofar as he felt that the more people he could get to testify that Louise Chorley was incapable of such an act as murder unless she was under the sort of stress that would render her insane, the better his hopes of convincing the jury.

As he had done yesterday, Maitland again looked for any sign from the prisoner that this witness was of special concern to her, and again he was disappointed. Louise Chorley continued to look straight ahead of her, apparently quite unconscious of her surroundings. And as the other character witnesses had done, Ernest Connolly shot one glance at her, and then looked firmly away. He seemed quite self-possessed, however, and answered O'Brien's questions readily enough.

As usual, Counsel began with the query as to how long the witness had known the accused. "Let's see," said Connolly. "My paper's been publishing her for fifteen years or so now, but she never came within my orbit until about six years ago I should say."

"But in that time you got to know her well?"

"Yes, I must say I did. You know her poems are very popular, with a certain section of the reading public that is. My wife happens to be one of her fans, she gave me no peace until I arranged that they should meet."

"Six years ago, I think you said?"

"The social meeting wouldn't be quite as long a time ago as that."

"But it was only the first of many occasions?"

"Yes, that's right. Of course, I saw her sometimes on business, but more often she and her husband would dine with us, and more often still she would get together with my wife, Maria, during the day."

"Thank you, Mr Connolly. Now I understand you have been a newspaperman for many years, a journalist before you took on your present editorial duties?"

"That's correct."

"Do you feel that this experience has given you a certain insight into human nature?"

"I suppose it must have done. But don't we all think that about ourselves?" added the witness rhetorically.

O'Brien chose to ignore that. "Tell me then, what do you think of my client, Mrs Louise Chorley?"

"I appreciate her professionalism, though the poems she writes are not exactly in my line."

"I was meaning as a person."

"That's more difficult." He took his time to think it over. "A sensitive person, devoted to her husband," he said at last.

"No friction in their relationship?" asked O'Brien quickly, making the most of what seemed to be an opportunity.

"I never observed any."

"Then may I ask you, Mr Connolly, do you think it likely that a lady such as you have described would be deceiving

166

her husband by carrying on an affaire outside her marriage?"

"No, I certainly do not."

"And there was no trouble between them to account for her having shot her husband?"

"Not while she was herself."

"In her right mind, you mean?"

"Yes, that's exactly what I do mean. It's impossible to imagine Louise with a gun in her hand."

"May I ask you, Mr Connolly, did you read the newspaper accounts of the inquest on David Chorley?"

"I did, and with interest. What happened – what seemed to have happened – wasn't the kind of thing that occurs to people one knows. Besides, my wife was very distressed about the whole business."

"You gathered then, I suppose, that Mrs Chorley had confessed to the murder?"

"Yes, I did."

"I think, with his lordship's permission," said O'Brien, though this had been tacitly given so many times before that the question hardly seemed necessary, "that I had better acquaint you, Mr Connolly, with the contents of her confession."

"What did she say?"

O'Brien once more repeated himself. "And was that all?" said Connolly, as though he was puzzled.

"Absolutely all. She steadfastly refused to give any further information – the man's name for instance. What conclusion would you put on that fact?"

"That he doesn't exist," said Connolly promptly.

"I think we have to admit that the organiser, as it seems most convenient to call him, is indeed a real person," said O'Brien, rather regretfully.

"That isn't what I meant. He may be real for all I know, and still Louise may have been imagining her connection with him."

"Do you think that's likely?"

"For an imaginative woman, yes. Her mind gave way under the strain of knowing what her husband had done," said Connolly, apparently improvising freely, and of course unaware of what had been said before in the

167

courtroom, "and then when she saw that he was dead she had a – a sort of reverse amnesia. I mean, instead of forgetting what she found unbearable she made up a story to explain it to herself."

"Thank you, Mr Connolly." O'Brien was genuinely grateful to the first of his witnesses to have put his own point of view to the jury without interference from the bench. "That is exactly the contention of the defence."

"Anyone knowing Louise—"

"And you knew her, you say, on a personal level, as well as a business associate?"

"The last is rather a pretentious way of putting it," said Connolly. "But certainly that is true."

"And you believe her incapable of having killed her husband coldbloodedly and of malice aforethought?"

"Indeed I do," said Connolly with emphasis.

O'Brien was so pleased with his witness that he ventured a further question. "The word Bohemian has been used in connection with my client," he said. "Would you say it is an apt one?"

"In the sense in which it is usually used, no, decidedly not. A little eccentricity in dress perhaps, no more than that."

"Thank you, Mr Connolly, that is all." O'Brien, not attempting to hide his satisfaction, sat down again. And Antony came to his feet.

"What was your opinion of David Chorley, Mr Connolly?" he asked.

"David? They were a mismatched couple in many ways."

"You said just now that Mrs Chorley was devoted to her husband."

"Yes, that's true. She was that sort of woman, who'd see it as her duty. But he was...rather a loud type of man."

"You don't think then that during the fifteen years of their marriage this loudness might have grated on her nerves?"

"No, I don't think so. I don't think she would allow it to."

"Ah yes, this question of being a dutiful wife that you spoke of. Now, Mr Connolly, out of this experience of

168

human nature that has been talked about, would you not agree that it's possible for someone of the sensitive, poetical nature that has been described also to have feelings of a very passionate kind? In fact," he went on quickly before the witness could answer, "don't you think such a woman might fall very deeply in love, perhaps at a little later age than most of us do?"

"Perhaps that's possible," Connolly conceded, "but you're looking at it from the woman's point of view only. What about the man?"

"You mustn't question counsel, Mr Connolly," said Carruthers gently.

"If your lordship pleases," said Maitland, "I should very much like to know exactly what the witness meant by that last remark."

"Very well, Mr Maitland. We will consider that you have asked him a question on those lines."

"Thank you, my lord. Well, Mr Connolly?"

The witness was obviously only too ready to answer. "I meant," he said, "look at her! I dare say she was quite good-looking as a girl, but would anybody want her now?"

Maitland was conscious of a furious muttering at his side from his learned leader. Certainly that last remark had been almost the most telling one made so far by any of O'Brien's character witnesses. He looked down for a moment at his notes without seeing them, and scandalised the judge and his own associate by saying to himself, but quite audibly, "All cats are grey at night."

"Mr Maitland!" said Carruthers, genuinely shocked, and let his eyes stray to where O'Brien was on his feet. "I quite agree with you, Mr O'Brien," he said courteously, "that remark has no place in the record."

"I am obliged to your lordship," said Kevin sanctimoniously, but there was a glint of amusement in his eye. Maitland turned back to the witness again.

"My friend for the defence has agreed to the existence of this organisation," he said, "and consequently to the existence of the man whom I have heard referred to somewhat fancifully as the spider in the centre of the web. Do you know Alan Kirby?"

169

For the first time Connolly's expression changed, and it was obvious that he had recognised the man who was questioning him. However, he contented himself with a simple answer, "Yes."

"There has been some discussion as to whether the picture he was accused of receiving had been stolen as part of the organisation's activities. Whether he was guilty or not is immaterial, the possibility I have outlined exists; and if that is the case his death is the third to be associated with this series of thefts."

"I suppose it is, but you can't blame Mrs Chorley for that."

"Certainly not, blame is no part of my function. I think that is all I have to ask you, Mr Connolly," he added consideringly, and sat down. Kevin O'Brien again declined to re-examine, which Halloran said was no wonder. He was getting things all his own way as it was.

"See if you can do any better with Connolly's wife," Antony suggested, but the comment was not well received.

Maria Connolly was another witness who might have been made precisely to Kevin O'Brien's specifications. Unlike her immediate predecessors, she seemed unable to take her eyes off the prisoner, who, however, still showed no sign at all of recognition. "I believe you were responsible for introducing your husband to my client, Mrs Louise Chorley," said O'Brien, after he had completed his preliminary questions.

"That's not quite right. He knew her already, through his work, you know. But I'd always been an admirer of hers, and I absolutely insisted that he let me meet her. After that we became close friends."

"Did you also know David Chorley?"

"Yes, but not so well. Louise and I would meet for lunch in town, or go to tea with each other."

"Can you tell me, even so, how their relationship struck you?"

"No different from anybody else's." For a moment her attention strayed back to Louise Chorley, and it was only O'Brien's clearing his throat that recalled her to the

170

question. "Men are all alike, aren't they? Always interested in what's going on outside the home. I know Ernest is, or he'd spend more time with us. I know the newspaper keeps him busy, but still if he really cared for the children and me—"

"Yes, Mrs Connolly, quite so. Are you implying that David Chorley was an inconsiderate husband?"

"Not particularly. Just like anybody else."

"And what was Mrs Chorley's attitude towards her marriage?"

"I always say there are worse things than being a spinster, but I don't know whether she looked on it like that or not. She was always very considerate of his feelings, and did everything to please him."

"Are you implying that she was frigid, Mrs Connolly?"

"Not exactly," said Maria, who also seemed to be taking her oath seriously. "Only that I think men care more for that sort of thing than women do." (Maitland waited for the judge to query the phrase, 'that sort of thing', but for a wonder he let it pass.)

"How, in your opinion, did Mrs Chorley regard her marriage vows?" asked O'Brien, a little taken aback by the witness's unpredictability.

"Oh, she was a very respectable woman." Again her look strayed towards Louise. "Is, I should say."

"And not the sort of lady to carry on an affaire outside her marriage?"

"Out of the question."

"There is, however, the question of her confession." Again O'Brien went into his explanation. "How do you account for that, Mrs Connolly?" (And he must be very sure of the answer he's going to get, thought Maitland, or he wouldn't keep putting that question quite so openly.)

"I don't believe a word of it," said Maria Connolly flatly.

"Perhaps you would explain that opinion a little."

"She has a beautiful soul," said Maria. "I don't really think I need say any more, need I? She'd never have done anything so – so mundane."

"But she has confessed to shooting her husband."

171

O'Brien was becoming more and more confident. "Can you explain that?"

"You say she'd just been hearing terrible things about him, her poor mind must have been turned, that's all. She'd never have done a thing like that – Louise with a gun! – if she'd had all her wits about her."

"And the explanation she gave for this act?"

"Imagination. Have you read any of her poems?"

"Yes," said O'Brien, concealing a slight shudder.

"Then you ought to understand. But you don't know her as well as I do. It's a wicked thing that she should be put through all this."

Having got on to a good thing, O'Brien had every intention of exploiting it. His questioning went on for quite a long time, without eliciting anything new. "Except," said Halloran sourly, as he rose to cross-examine, "that Louise Chorley had some damned good friends."

"As you have explained to us, Mrs Connolly," he said blandly to the witness, "the Chorley household was not altogether a happy one."

"As good as most," said Maria, reminding Antony all at once of a gramophone record that had become stuck in one groove.

"But you, Mrs Connolly, have not the best of opinions of marriage as an institution, I believe?"

"It might be worse," said Maria grudgingly. "On the other hand, it might be a good deal better."

"Then do you really think it's necessary for us to make all these esoteric guesses as to what went on in Louise Chorley's mind before she shot her husband? Would it not be simpler to say that they got on each other's nerves for years, and she couldn't stand it any longer? Particularly in view of what she had just learned about him."

"I know that kind of thing happens, but not to Louise."

"It never occurred to you that she might have some interest outside the home? Mrs Connolly!" he added sharply, as the witness's attention seemed to stray to the woman in the dock again.

"What did you say? Oh yes! Well, there was her poetry, of course."

"Yes, I know all about that. I meant an interest of a personal nature."

"Louise wasn't that sort of a woman," said Maria firmly. "But I can imagine her making up that story and then believing it was true. If she was sufficiently upset, of course."

And there Halloran had to leave it, though it wasn't for want of trying. He was well aware of the effect on the jury that these character witnesses, with their unanimity about Louise Chorley in spite of the different angles from which they viewed her, must have had. Maria Connolly was unshakeable, the only one of the lot who really loved Louise, in Maitland's opinion; Hilda Kirby was a charitable woman, and the rest of them – except one – had spoken as they believed, but it was from a sense of duty, not from real affection.

So the luncheon adjournment passed in a good deal of fruitless discussion. By one-thirty they were back in court and Kevin O'Brien was calling his final witness, his client herself.

There had been some speculation between Halloran and Maitland as to how Louise Chorley would conduct herself when she got into the witness-box. O'Brien must be confident that she had something to say for herself, or he wouldn't be calling her; on the other hand she'd been completely silent and passive until now. In the event she allowed the wardress to conduct her from the dock and across the court-room, and it wasn't until she had the bible in her hand that she showed some sign of comprehending what was going on. She looked down at it then and said, as if to the world at large, "I was always taught as a child to tell the truth. Do I have to swear to it?"

For a moment Kevin O'Brien was a little taken aback, obviously he had not expected that question. "It is open to you to affirm your testimony, Mrs Chorley," he explained.

"Oh no, the bible is for people who believe," said Louise. "Thou shalt not take the name of the Lord thy God in vain," she added vaguely. "Therefore I must certainly take an oath."

"Very well, Mrs Chorley." He signalled to the usher who was standing by patiently.

"Take the book in your right hand—"

She repeated the well-worn formula quietly but respectfully. Maitland and Halloran exchanged a puzzled look. "Now, Mrs Chorley, I have to ask you, do you understand the nature of these proceedings?" said Kevin O'Brien.

"When someone is killed there has to be a trial," said Louise. "David was killed, and so—" Her voice trailed off into a murmur, and then she added more strongly, "You see, he knew too much."

"Just a moment, Mrs Chorley." A little of O'Brien's confidence was oozing away. "You have been sitting here very quietly these last few days. Have you been listening to what was said?"

"I didn't want to hear it," she told him, almost childishly.

"Still, I think certain things must have impressed themselves on you."

"Oh yes." She gave the impression of being only too willing to agree with him.

"And did you understand the things you heard?"

"I think so," she said doubtfully.

"You understand, then, what we want to hear from you. Exactly how it came about that you shot your husband."

"It's a very long story," she said and looked around her as though realising for the first time how many people there were in the court. "I told you once — don't you remember? — and I told the police when they came after David was dead, and then I wrote it down, for the newspaper."

"Yes, Mrs Chorley, but you see these good people, the members of the jury, would like to hear it now from your own lips. Come now," O'Brien added, putting forward all his charm in a way that would have made Maitland, before he understood his colleague as well as he did now, have labelled him a charlatan. "You shall tell us in your own words, I won't even interrupt you if you prefer it that way. And you may take all the time that is necessary."

174

"Very well," she said. "It was all so simple, you know. David knew everything, I couldn't let him hurt my beloved. I had to stop that somehow."

"Perhaps if you go back a little, Mrs Chorley," O'Brien suggested.

"I knew from the beginning, as soon as I saw Him, how much there was between us. I knew that we were capable of an ideal relationship, one that nothing in the world could spoil. We couldn't live together openly, the world doesn't understand these things, and both of us were married, but He arranged everything so that what we had was perfection. He was always so very good to me, what He was doing didn't matter, He had a right to the beautiful things, to everything the world could give Him, and when I was with Him, my beloved, heaven touched me too. But David knew, and when I realised he was going to tell the police everything... what else could I do but kill him?"

Kevin O'Brien was looking happier now, he seemed to have got his client's wavelength. "You fetched the gun," he prompted.

"Oh yes, while he was writing his confession that he had killed poor Emily Walpole."

"And when you came back you shot him. Did you realise, I wonder, at that time that what you were doing was wrong?"

Maitland found himself holding his breath, waiting for the answer. It was a daring question, and he wondered whether he himself would have taken the chance. But there was nothing to worry about, from the defence's point of view at least. "Wrong?" said Louise Chorley, questioningly. "I don't know what you mean. How could it be wrong to do away with somebody who would have harmed Him, my beloved? I thought no more of it than I would have done about squashing an earwig."

"You had heard what the detectives had to say to your husband earlier that day, had you not, Mrs Chorley?"

"Yes, I was there for part of the time when they were questioning him."

"It was a shock to you, I imagine, to learn that he had been involved not only in the crime of murder but in that of theft?"

"Oh no, oh no. He was beside me all the time, telling me what to do."

"He, Mrs Chorley?"

"My beloved. Don't you understand me, this was something that had to be done? When the thought of the gun came into my mind I knew that He had put it there. Everything followed quite naturally after that."

O'Brien threw one quick glance at the jury, seemed satisfied with what he saw, and turned back to his client again. "Thank you, Mrs Chorley, I shall not worry you any further this afternoon. I'm afraid you must stay there, though, for just a little while longer. My learned friend may have some questions for you."

Halloran was half way to his feet when he felt Maitland's hand on his arm and plunged back into his place again. "What is it now?" he asked, not too pleased with the interruption.

"Let me!" Antony pleaded. He couldn't think of anything else to say, but his expression and the words were urgent enough.

"We agreed –" Halloran started. And then, suspiciously, "What have you in mind?"

"I can't explain now. You'll see."

"That's what I'm afraid of. Oh, very well then," said Halloran, as gruff as Maitland had ever heard him. And added as the younger man got up swiftly, "And Heaven help you if you make a mess of it."

But Maitland had already forgotten him, his whole attention absorbed by the witness. He was perfectly certain now, after the way she had told her story – which had been clever, damnably clever – that there was scarcely a person in court who believed she had ever had a lover. The question was, how to set about getting some sensible responses from her, something that would convince the jury of her sanity? And then, if possible, to learn the name that so far had eluded him, the name of the spider at the centre of the web, the name of Alan Kirby's killer, the man who had frightened Jenny.

"How did your husband, David Chorley, come to be involved in the art thefts?" he asked, rather abruptly.

She looked at him as though with incomprehension. "I

176

don't know," she said, "how should I know a thing like that?"

"I think you know very well, Mrs Chorley." Heaven help him, and the prosecution too, if the jury thought he was bullying her. "I think you felt he'd be a useful recruit, and suggested his name to this lover of yours. You'd do anything to help him, wouldn't you?"

"Oh yes, I would."

"And David had a certain characteristic that hasn't been mentioned during this hearing. He was a man who loved adventure, who loved taking chances. May I suggest to you that when he discovered your liaison you got him the offer of this job – shall we call it? – as a sop to his pride."

"I don't think you understand at all. He was so far beneath us – "

"Isn't that how it happened, Mrs Chorley?"

"Something like that, perhaps," she said, shaking her head, so that her admission did nothing to dispel the impression she had been conveying.

"Did you know that Alan Kirby is dead?" asked Maitland, again changing direction abruptly.

"Alan? Oh no!" He took heart from the fact that that was the first genuine sign of emotion he had managed to wring from her.

"He'd been accused of receiving stolen goods," said Antony. He knew perfectly well that she was aware of this already, but the point must be made to the court. "To be precise, a painting by Rubens. Before the case came to trial he was gunned down in the street near his home."

"I'm so sorry about that," she whimpered.

"Now I don't know how it seems to you, Mrs Chorley, but it's very apparent to me that the art thefts and his death are somehow connected. If this was done either by or at the instigation of your lover, don't you think it's time he was stopped?"

"If... no, I can't believe it. But if it was His doing," she said, recovering herself, "there must have been a good reason. He has a perfect right to take any action He wishes." As before she spoke of the man she called her beloved reverently, as though she was referring to the deity.

177

"The right of life and death over his fellow mortals?" Maitland was beginning, when he became conscious of a stir in the quiet room and a piece of paper was shoved along the desk in front of him. "More notes," he heard Halloran mutter angrily beside him, but he was aware of the quick stirring of excitement and could afford to ignore his leader.

"With your permission, my lord," he said.

"I think Mrs Chorley will forgive you if you delay your questions for a little," said Carruthers dryly.

"I'm grateful to your lordship." He was unfolding the sheet of paper as he spoke. On it there was just an address, that and nothing more, but when he looked across the court to where the previous witnesses were sitting he was able to catch Sykes's eye and received a nod which he took to indicate encouragement.

"I wonder, Mrs Chorley," – Maitland's eyes were still on the sheet of paper – "how often did you visit Apartment 408, Brinkley Court?" And as he finished he looked up suddenly and saw the prisoner's hands clench on the rail in front of her until the knuckles showed white, and caught too the momentary flash of undoubted intelligence in her eyes.

"So He didn't – " she said, as though she couldn't help herself, and then was silent.

"No, Mrs Chorley, he didn't stop using it after you went to prison," said Maitland slowly. "Did you think he was the kind of man who would content himself with the company of a wife he despised?"

"I don't know what you mean," she said defiantly.

"My lord!" said Counsel for the Defence.

"You have something you wish to communicate, Mr O'Brien?" asked the judge.

"Indeed I have, my lord. This is not – "

"If you're about to say it isn't relevant, I'm afraid I can't agree with you. It is a little difficult to tell until the matter has been probed further, but I think it may be very relevant indeed."

"If your lordship pleases." O'Brien's tone was very faintly mutinous.

"You may return to your cross-examination, Mr Maitland," said Carruthers in his courteous way.

Now that the wind has been taken out my sails, now that she's forewarned of the line on which I propose to attack her, thought Maitland, but he expressed his gratitude as gracefully as though none of these ideas had ever crossed his mind. When he turned back to the witness, his tone was casual. "Do you know on what theory your counsel is basing your defence?" he asked.

The vague look was back again, more pronounced than ever now. "I had a right to kill David," she said.

"Come now, Mrs Chorley, you can't tell me Mr O'Brien didn't explain to you very clearly exactly what the issues were." ("Thank you for nothing," O'Brien muttered.)

"He talked to me for a very long time," said Louise in a fading voice. "I suppose he meant well, but I don't think he ever really understood that anything He needed doing just had to be done."

"Then I'll try and explain it to you myself," said Antony, still in the same quiet tone. "Perhaps I'll have better fortune than my learned friend."

"I think perhaps you might, Mr Maitland."

That was an admission of a sort. She had been alert enough to pick up his name from the exchanges he had had with the judge; or perhaps she had recognised him, in spite of the disguising wig and gown, in spite of their brief acquaintance six months and more ago. "The contention is that you knew nothing of your husband's activities until the morning of his death, that the knowledge affected your reason, and so you shot him. And because this was against your nature, that gentle, spiritual, poetical, sensitive nature that we have heard so much about, you invented the story of a mythical lover to explain your actions to yourself, a story that is all fantasy."

"Oh, no, no. David was a crass man, but that wasn't why I killed him. I had to, can't I make you understand that?"

"You had to because of your lover, who was the head of the organisation which you must have heard discussed so often in this very court?"

"Yes, yes, of course." She cast an agonised glance at her

179

counsel, but O'Brien was silent. Antony was again conscious of the sudden prick of excitement, but it was accompanied now by a very poignant feeling of regret.

"You do realise, don't you, Mrs Chorley," he said, "that if you want us to believe in this man you'll have to tell us his name? Do you really think it's worth while to shield him any longer?" His voice had quickened now. "Remember what he said about you: *I dare say she was quite good looking as a girl, but would anybody want her now?* Can you believe after that that the whole affaire wasn't based on a lie, that you were useful to him, if only because he craved companionship in the second part of the double life he was leading? Do you really believe he's spending those stolen evenings alone now? You're standing where you are because you tried to shield him, but do you think he cares at all?"

"Oh yes, he existed all right." She spoke in a hard voice, and the rather fey manner had gone. Apart from her words the court-room was suddenly very quiet, and in the silence Maitland realised, with surprisingly little pleasure, that his part was played and he had won.

"He's here, isn't he, Mrs Chorley?" he asked gently.

"Of course he is," she said scornfully. "And I think you know his name perfectly well, though I can't understand how you guessed it. Ernest Connolly, though we were Mr and Mrs Campbell at Brinkley Court. He said he loved me." Just for a moment her voice broke on something very like a sob, but then it came strongly again. "Yes, I loved him, and, yes, I killed for him. Not in shock and horror as you thought, Mr Attorney," – she turned and almost spat the words at O'Brien – "but after I'd thought it out it seemed the only thing to do. I never cared for David anyway. And, fool that I was, I'd have done anything for Ernest." She threw up her hands suddenly, and it was hard to tell whether the gesture was despairing, or whether – perhaps, after all, the same thing – she was symbolically relinquishing her hold on life. "And he can't even keep faithful to my memory six months!" she said, and it never occurred to anyone, as a sudden hubbub broke out among the spectators, that the words were in any way an anti-climax.

180

Thursday, after the verdict

"What happened after that?" asked Jenny faintly when he reached that part of his narrative that evening. Sir Nicholas and Vera were with them – a transference of the traditional Tuesday evening dinner – and Kevin O'Brien, too, had been invited to share the meal. They were still drinking their before-dinner sherry, and Antony did not reply until he had replenished their glasses, moving stiffly as he did when he was tired.

"Halloran took over," he said shortly, as he sat down again.

"But this man Connolly, surely he was in the court?"

"Of course he was, love. But so was Sykes, and I learned later that he had a few minions posted outside. Anyway, there wasn't a riot, if that's what you mean."

"Perhaps I can finish the story," Kevin offered. "I wasn't dissatisfied with the verdict, even though it went against me –"

"You mean," Jenny insisted, "they found her Guilty, with no extenuating circumstances?"

"Yes, Jenny, that's what I mean. She'd never taken me in for a moment, of course, with that act of hers, but still those were my instructions, I had to do my best with what she gave me."

"Very proper," said Sir Nicholas and Vera together.

"Thank you." There was some amusement in O'Brien's tone, which seemed mainly to be self-directed. "After the outburst that Antony has described, she went on to tell us the whole story. The whole true story."

"That's exactly what we want to hear," said Jenny, who seemed in a very demanding mood that evening. "But first I want to know what happened to Mr Connolly. After all he tried to kill Antony, didn't he?"

"I think there's no doubt about that, though, of course, that was something outside the scope of Louise Chorley's knowledge. He's helping the police with their enquiries,"

181

said Kevin. "Does that make you happy, Jenny? I think there's no doubt at all that an arrest will follow."

"All right, then you can tell us the rest," said Jenny, sitting back and folding her hands in her lap to signify that she was now ready to listen.

"There isn't really very much to tell. One thing I think was obvious: Mrs Chorley took these poems of hers very seriously, and was constantly acting out the role of – how was it that you put it, Antony? – a sensitive, rather spiritual person, which completely deceived most of her friends. The affair with Connolly had been going on almost as long as they had known each other, and I think there's no doubt that it was a pretty intense business. They must have both been incredibly discreet, because the police never got a sniff of the Brinkley Court address until you suggested to Sykes that Connolly should be followed, Antony. They had heard the name Campbell, I now understand, but had no Christian name or initial to go on, and nothing to connect it with any particular address. If they'd had anything more definite . . . But can you imagine tracking down every Campbell in the phone book, on the vague chance they might be involved in something criminal? Do you know Brinkley Court at all, any of you?"

"I've walked past it," said Antony. "I always imagined it was the last word in luxury."

"And you were right. I have an aunt who lives there," Kevin explained, "that's how I know. Anyway, according to Mrs Chorley, Connolly maintained it as a love nest. I'm sorry Lady Harding," he apologised, "she'd played her part so long she was still addicted to clichés. But I think it had a great use for him too as a headquarters from which he could run his organisation, with nobody at all knowing his real name. And I think too that he could spend his money as he liked there – his ill-gotten gains as Louise would doubtless have said if she'd thought of it – and it will be found, for instance, that there are paintings – bought or stolen, I don't know – that he wouldn't have dreamed of displaying in his own home."

"His own home was pretty austere," said Antony.

"Exactly what I would have expected. If I were making

lots of money illegally," said Kevin, rather wistfully, "I wouldn't go about openly displaying my wealth, I'd collect it like a – spider was your word Antony, wasn't it? – and make a run for it when I thought I had enough."

"Well, you know," Maitland conceded, "that's probably what he intended to do. There was obviously no love lost between him and his wife, and I couldn't see any sign that he cared for his children at all either."

"All this," said Sir Nicholas suddenly interrupting them, "is pure speculation."

"Deduction, I think," said O'Brien pensively. "And, of course, the part that Louise Chorley told us about their affaire isn't speculation at all."

"No, I'll give you that much," said Sir Nicholas grudgingly.

"Two questions," said Vera. "Did David Chorley know what was going on, and when did Louise learn that her lover was a criminal?"

"Louise said David knew but didn't care," said Kevin. "I don't know whether that was true or not. And she wasn't a foolish woman, you know; I think she realised early on that Connolly wasn't running two establishments on his salary as one of *The Courier*'s editors. Particularly with the second one being at a place like Brinkley Court. I'm sure she made it her business to find out, and she was so far genuine in the tale she told that she was quite ready to accept any activity of his. And if that wasn't clever, to tell the exact truth, but embellish it so that it sounded like a lie, I don't know the meaning of the word. So I think, as you were able to convince the court, Antony, that she was perfectly sane in her attitude towards him."

"I don't think I did much convincing," said Maitland. "She did it all herself."

"Yes, that's quite true, once you got her going. Does that answer your questions, Lady Harding?"

"Quite satisfactorily," Vera told him. "So when David Chorley was recruited into the organisation –?"

"I've been wondering about that," said Antony. "If he knew what his wife was up to, that she had a lover I mean, he might have welcomed the chance to make the extra

183

money, in the hope of winning her back and being able to offer her a more comfortable way of life."

"Will nothing stop you?" Sir Nicholas's question was obviously rhetorical. "You're guessing again," he said accusingly.

"Yes, I agree. All we really know is that she did invite David's help, that he did accept one or more assignments, and that later he killed Emily Walpole to protect himself. Now, that's an idea," he added, with sudden animation. "Suppose he didn't. Suppose it was Connolly who killed her, for some reason we know nothing about."

"My dear boy," Sir Nicholas's tone was suspiciously gentle, "I am quite ready to accept the very circumstantial case you made out against David Chorley at the time, which was confirmed, let me remind you, by evidence uncovered by the police."

"So it was. To get back to his murder, I've told you everything that Mrs Chorley said about that day."

"And your client, Mr O'Brien," said Vera, "is on her way to prison. Hope you don't mind too much."

"On the contrary, I believe, with Halloran, that she's better off there than under a psychiatrist's care. They have this nasty habit," he added, looking round at the others, "of releasing their patients on an unsuspecting world far too soon."

"This is where we came in," said Antony, but he said it for Jenny's ear alone.

"Lost your case," Vera pointed out. She seemed to have taken a fancy to O'Brien.

"So I did. But it isn't the first time and it won't be the last," said Kevin philosophically. "In fact," he added – and any of the others in the room could have told him the remark was tactless – "I think I'm happier in losing than Antony is in having won."

"Halloran is happy," said Sir Nicholas idly, intent on creating a diversion. "He got his verdict, and he says it was largely your doing, Antony."

"Magnanimous, if untrue," said Maitland. He didn't look as if he relished the compliment.

But it was one thing for someone outside the family circle to say something that might offend his nephew's sensibilities, quite another for Sir Nicholas himself to do so. "Credit where credit is due," he said unkindly. He knew well enough that though Maitland would rather see the guilty in prison than the innocent, he was hard put to it to reconcile himself to the existence of those dreary institutions at all. "I shouldn't be surprised if this led to some more work of the same nature. Mallory was saying—"

Antony, who had been doing his best to look relaxed for Jenny's sake, sat up suddenly very straight. "Uncle Nick, he wouldn't dare," he said indignantly.

"Why not? I think—"

"Don't tease him," interrupted Vera gruffly.

For once Sir Nicholas allowed himself a sense of outrage at something his wife had said. "I never teased anybody in my life," he retorted austerely.

"You do it all the time," said Jenny, who had had an anxious eye on her husband all the evening. It was surprising, and very gratifying, that he had recovered from what Mr Justice Carruthers had called his indisposition with so little sign of ill effect; it wasn't his physical state that worried her, but his state of mind. She'd never known a time yet when there hadn't been a reaction to a scene such as the one played that day in court, though she also knew that he would have been even more uneasy if Alan Kirby's death hadn't been avenged. "There's still a lot I don't understand," she said now. "You gave Inspector Sykes—"

"Chief Inspector," corrected her husband automatically.

"— the name of one of your suspects, and asked him to find out if the man had a second residence."

"I must admit I didn't expect any results from that," said Antony. "It was pure luck that Connolly visited Brinkley Court during the luncheon recess. Of course, it took Sykes's chap a little time to get a message to the Chief Inspector. But I was glad to see it when it did come."

"Yes, that's all very well, but how did you know?" asked Jenny. "According to what Alan Kirby told you it might have been any of the three, and I know at one time you thought his uncle Daniel was much the most likely."

"In one way he was." (Jenny had been quite right, her husband's mood improved as he gave his mind to the problem.) "But in another way, the fact that he was such a connoisseur of art, absolutely mad about it, could be taken both ways."

"Can't you give us a single sentence without resorting to colloquialisms?" asked Sir Nicholas disagreeably. But he followed the query rather quickly with another. "How do you mean, might be taken in two ways?"

"Could he have borne to part with his treasures?"

"The answer to that is, I don't know, and neither do you," said his uncle flatly.

"No, but it's a point to bear in mind. Also, I think Ernest Connolly's display of comparative penury was a point against him. The organiser, who presumably was making a good deal of money out of his efforts, might have been chary about displaying the fact that he was a wealthy man. As Kevin pointed out."

"If that's all you had to go on—"

"No, I only thought about that later. Though even when I conducted those first interviews on Alan Kirby's behalf, it did strike me that his uncle, Daniel Kirby, was very open about his feelings, about the art thefts, about everything I asked him, in fact. The same thing applied, to a lesser extent, to Raymond Shields. But there were two much more important points. Ernest Connolly was the only one who didn't mention being called as a character witness for Louise Chorley until I asked him the question directly, even though her name had been mentioned. That didn't seem natural. But even more telling was the fact that he was the only one who seemed to have heard of my connection with the Selden case, which as you know was never mentioned in the press. I didn't see how he could have heard that except from Louise herself. Then later, in court, I made a point of mentioning to each of the three men the fact that three deaths had resulted from the organiser's activities. Daniel Kirby and Raymond Shields both reacted to the statement with surprise, Connolly was the only one who didn't query the statement, and I am pretty sure that was because he had killed Alan himself, and also the man called Nobby Clark whom Sykes had

186

mentioned to me." He paused there, as though he had nothing more to say.

"Can't leave it at that," Vera said emphatically.

"I thought everything was quite clear now."

"Not exactly," his uncle told him. "Was Alan Kirby a part of the conspiracy? And did his death arise from that fact?"

"That's something I can't answer, though if you want me to guess—"

"Must you?" enquired Sir Nicholas.

"I was only going to say I believe him to have been innocent," said Antony. "In a way," he added moodily, "I wish I didn't. But why anyone should have wanted to frame him, I haven't the faintest idea."

"Nor why he was killed, I suppose."

"Do you want me to use my imagination again, Uncle Nick? All right then, I think he probably knew, or discovered too much about Ernest Connolly. But what sort of a thing that might have been I don't know; probably something apparently innocuous, or he'd have mentioned it to me."

"Not a very satisfactory conclusion," he said much later to Jenny, when the others had gone.

"You did what you set out to do," said Jenny stoutly. "You unmasked your spider, and—"

"Don't mix your metaphors, love. Besides, if you think about it, we still don't know for sure that he killed Alan Kirby," Antony pointed out.

"I think we can assume he did."

"Yes, but don't let Uncle Nick hear you say that, love. And I'd still like to know—" But before he could complete the sentence the telephone rang.

It was Chief Inspector Sykes, and what with his apologies for calling at such a late hour, and his punctilious enquiries about everyone's health, the conversation took some time. Antony turned from the phone at last, and said, still with his hand on the receiver, "The answers to all our questions, Jenny love. Do you want to hear?"

"Of course I do!"

187

"All right then. It won't take long, but I think I could do with another drink before I start."

"I'll get you one," said Jenny obligingly. She was itching to know what he had to say, but wisely refrained from demanding an instant explanation. "There!" she said after a moment. "Sit down Antony, and we can be comfortable."

Her husband, however, had wandered over to the fireplace, and placed his glass on the mantel near the clock. "You can stop worrying, love," he said, turning to face her. "Ernest Connolly has confessed to murdering Alan, so you don't need to worry about him any more."

"I wasn't worrying," Jenny lied.

"Come now, love, I know you better than that. You were afraid they'd release him, and he'd want his revenge," he added as dramatically as he could.

"It's all very well trying to ridicule the idea, but you must admit something like that might have happened," said Jenny. "But that wasn't all Inspector Sykes told you, surely?"

"Not quite. He gave me the answer to our two remaining questions, which he had from Connolly as part of his statement."

"You mean, why Alan was framed?"

"For one thing. It was quite simple really, he knew – or thought he knew – where Connolly lived."

"What do you mean?"

"He saw him going into Brinkley Court one day, and happened to mention the fact the next time they met. He had no idea Connolly was known under a different name there, of course, or that he wasn't living there with his wife and children. That's why he never mentioned it to me, it wasn't important. But Connolly thought he'd be better out of the way. You can imagine he felt fairly jittery after Louise killed her husband."

"And when he killed Alan, was it still to prevent him telling about Brinkley Court?"

"No, though it would have been a good enough motive. Sykes says a number of stolen paintings were found in the apartment there, I think that was what made Connolly open his mouth finally. He'd been maintaining that Louise

188

Chorley was as mad as a hatter, but once he knew the police had identified him as the organiser he didn't seem to care about anything else. All that really mattered to him were his possessions."

"You still haven't told me," said Jenny, with a sense of strong foreboding, "why he killed Alan."

"No, love, because you won't like it. I don't like it much myself. He knew I was asking questions on young Kirby's behalf, and thought that way he could shut my mouth. And he might have succeeded, you know. I'd no shadow of right to ask any more questions once my client was dead, and if Uncle Nick and Halloran between them hadn't taken a hand—"

"Antony, don't worry so. You were trying to help Alan Kirby."

"I know I was. I did my best," said Antony bitterly, "and see what came of it."

"I think," said Jenny slowly, "that Alan might have been killed in any case."

"How do you make that out?"

"I think," said Jenny, and suddenly she was talking eagerly, with far more confidence than was usual with her, "I think that he was killed because Ernest Connolly had been called as a character witness at Mrs Chorley's trial. Don't you think he must have been petrified about that? He couldn't have heard a word from her since she was arrested, and knew nothing about the sort of defence Kevin was going to put on. He'd be more than ever eager that no one should know a thing about Brinkley Court."

"That's all very well, but it isn't what he told Sykes."

"No, but don't you see, Antony, he must hate you now? Wouldn't he have said that just to hurt you?"

Maitland took his time to think that out. Then he picked up his glass, sipped his cognac, and went to sit beside his wife on the sofa. "You know, love, something tells me you may be right about that. And I've had another thought; perhaps Louise didn't sell her story to *The Courier* just so that they'd pay for her defence. She may not have realised they couldn't use it until the verdict was in and have thought of it as a way to get a message to that wretched man, to assure him that she'd never give him away."

189

"But she did in the end," said Jenny soberly.

"At my instigation, don't forget that. However, about this theory of yours, Jenny love – as we've no possible way of knowing, let's pretend it's the truth."

"Let's," said Jenny with enthusiasm, and slid her hand into his. Meeting her eyes, he saw that hers had again their untroubled look, and was comforted.